The Mystery
of the
TALKING
SKULL

Alfred Hitchcock and
The Three Investigators in

The Mystery
of the
TALKING
SKULL

by Robert Arthur

Cover by Harry Kane

SCHOLASTIC INC.
NEW YORK · TORONTO · LONDON · AUCKLAND · SYDNEY · TOKYO

ISBN 0-590-36001-9

12 11 10 9 8 7 6 5 4 3   3 4 5 6 7/8

Printed in the U.S.A.   01

CONTENTS

A SHORT PREVIEW
BY ALFRED HITCHCOCK

Welcome, mystery lovers! We are gathered together again for another stimulating case of The Three Investigators, whose official motto is "We Investigate Anything." If they had known what they were getting into when they tackled the curious case of the talking skull they might have changed their motto.

Be that as it may, they find themselves this time in a mix-up of mystery and danger which leads them from one perplexing enigma to another until — but I am not a blabbermouth. I promised faithfully not to tell too much, and I shall keep my promise.

Indeed, I shall only say that The Three Investigators are Jupiter Jones, Pete Crenshaw, and Bob Andrews, who all make their home in Rocky Beach, a small municipality in California a few miles from Hollywood. Their headquarters is a mobile home trailer in The Jones Salvage Yard, a superjunkyard owned by Jupiter's aunt and uncle, Mr. and Mrs. Titus Jones.

The boys make an excellent team. Jupiter has a quick mind and is adept at deductions. Pete is less intellectual but sturdy and courageous. Bob is somewhat studious and an excellent researcher. Together they have solved some very intriguing mysteries indeed.

Which is all I shall say at this time, for I know you are eager to dispense with this preview and get to the main feature.

Alfred Hitchcock

JUPITER BUYS A TRUNK

It all started because Jupiter Jones read the newspaper.

The Three Investigators — Jupiter, Pete Crenshaw, and Bob Andrews — were taking it easy back in Jupe's workshop section of The Jones Salvage Yard. Bob was writing up some notes on their last case. Pete was just enjoying the California morning sunshine. And Jupiter was reading the paper.

Presently he looked up from its pages.

"Has either of you ever been to an auction?" he asked.

Bob said no. Pete shook his head.

"Neither have I," Jupiter said. "The paper

says there's an auction this morning at the Davis Auction Company in Hollywood. They'll be auctioning off to the highest bidder unclaimed luggage from a number of hotels. The paper says there are trunks and suitcases with unknown contents, left behind by people who moved, or couldn't pay their bill, or who just forgot to call for them. I think it might be interesting to visit an auction."

"Why?" Pete asked. "I don't need a suitcase full of somebody's old clothes."

"Neither do I," Bob said. "Let's go swimming."

"We should seek out new experiences," Jupiter said. "Every new experience helps broaden our background as investigators. I'll see if Uncle Titus will let Hans drive us up to Hollywood in the light truck."

Hans, one of two Bavarian brothers who helped in the salvage yard, was free. And so, an hour later, the boys were standing in a large room crowded with people, watching a short, plump auctioneer on a raised platform auction off trunks and suitcases as rapidly as possible. At the moment he had a new-looking suitcase in front of him and was trying to get one more bid on it.

"Going once! Going once!" he shouted.

2

"Going twice! Going twice!...Gone! Sold for twelve dollars and fifty cents to the gentleman with the red necktie."

The auctioneer banged his gavel, signifying that the sale was final. Then he turned to see what came next.

"Now we come to lot 98!" he sang out. "A very interesting item, ladies and gentlemen. Interesting and unusual. Hoist it up where everyone can see it, boys."

Two sturdy workmen lifted a small, old-fashioned trunk onto the platform. Pete stirred restlessly. It was a hot day and the room was stuffy. Some of the men present seemed quite interested in bidding on the unknown contents of the luggage, but Pete couldn't have cared less.

"C'mon, Jupe, let's go!" Pete muttered to his stocky companion.

"Just a little longer," Jupe whispered back. "This looks like an interesting item. I think I'll bid on it."

"On that?" Pete stared at the trunk. "You're crazy."

"Just the same, I think I'll try to buy it. If it's worth anything, we'll all share."

"Worth anything? It's probably full of clothes that went out of style in 1890," Bob said.

The trunk indeed looked old. It was made of wood, with leather straps and leather binding, and had a rounded top. It looked stoutly locked.

"Ladies and gentlemen," the auctioneer shouted, "I invite your attention to this fine trunk. Believe me, folks, they don't make trunks like this one anymore!"

A snicker went through the crowd. It was certainly true no one made trunks like that anymore. The trunk could easily have been fifty years old.

"I think it's an old actor's trunk," Jupe whispered to his two companions. "The kind actors touring in plays used to take with them to keep their costumes in."

"One thing we don't need is a bunch of old costumes," Pete muttered back. "For gosh sake, Jupe — "

But the auctioneer was already shouting his sales talk.

"Look at it, ladies and gentlemen, look at it!" he cried. "Not new, not modern, no indeed. But think of it as an antique. Think of it as a fond memento of grandfather's day. And what may be in it?"

He rapped the trunk with his knuckles. It gave off a dull thud.

"Who knows what it holds? It might hold anything. Why, folks, the crown jewels of the former czars of old Russia might be in that trunk. I don't guarantee it, but certainly the possibility can't be denied. Now what am I bid? Give me an offer, someone. Give me an offer."

The crowd was silent. Apparently no one wanted an old trunk. The auctioneer looked annoyed.

"Come on, folks!" he implored. "Give me a bid! Let's get this started. This fine old antique trunk, this precious relic of yesterday, this — "

He was just getting wound up in his spiel when Jupiter Jones took a step forward.

"One dollar!" he called, his voice squeaking slightly with excitement.

"One dollar!" the auctioneer interrupted himself to shout. "I have one dollar from that intelligent-looking young man in the first row. And you know what I'm going to do, folks? I'm going to reward this intelligence by selling it to him for one dollar! Sold!"

And he brought his gavel down hard. The crowd chuckled. No one else wanted the trunk, and the auctioneer wasn't wasting time trying to get any more bids. Now Jupiter Jones was the somewhat surprised owner of one antique trunk, tightly locked, contents unknown.

At that moment, however, there was a stir in

the back of the crowd. A woman was trying to push her way through — a little old lady with white hair, an old-fashioned hat, and gold-rimmed spectacles.

"Wait a minute!" she called. "I want to bid. Ten dollars! I bid ten dollars for the trunk!"

People turned to look at her, surprised at anyone wanting to pay ten dollars for such an old trunk.

"Twenty dollars!" the white-haired woman called, waving her hand. "I'll bid twenty dollars!"

"I'm sorry, madam," the auctioneer called back. "The article has been sold and all sales are final. Take it away, men, take it away. We have to get on with the sale."

The two workmen lifted the trunk down from the platform, swinging it toward The Three Investigators.

"Here you are," one said. Pete and Jupiter stepped forward.

"Well, it looks as if we own one old trunk," Pete grumbled, seizing a leather handle at one end. "Now what'll we do with it?"

"Take it back to the salvage yard and open it," Jupe said, grasping the leather handle at the other end.

"Wait a minute, fellows," the second workman said. "First it has to be paid for. Mustn't forget that important detail."

"Oh, that's right." Jupe put down his end, reached in his pocket for a leather wallet, took out a dollar bill, and handed it to the man. The man scribbled on a paper and gave it to Jupe.

"Your receipt," he said. "Now it's yours. If there're any royal jewels in it, you own them. Haw haw!" Still laughing, he let the boys take the trunk. With Bob ahead of them, pushing a way through the crowd, Jupe and Pete carried the small trunk toward the rear of the room. They had just got it through the rows of people when the white-haired woman who had come too late to bid bustled up to them.

"Boys," she said, "I'll buy that trunk from you for twenty-five dollars. I collect old trunks and I want this one for my collection."

"Gosh, twenty-five dollars!" Pete exclaimed.

"Take it, Jupe!" Bob said.

"It's a very good profit, and the trunk isn't really worth a cent more even to a collector," the woman said. "Here you are, twenty-five dollars."

She took the money from a large pocketbook and thrust it at Jupiter. To the amazement of Bob and Pete, Jupiter shook his head.

"I'm sorry, ma'am," he said. "We don't want

7

to sell it. We want to see what's in it."

"There can't be anything in it of value," the woman said, looking upset. "Here, I'll give you thirty dollars."

"No, thank you." Jupiter shook his head again. "I really don't want to sell it."

The woman sighed. Then, just as she was about to say something more, she seemed to take alarm. She turned and scurried away, losing herself in the crowd. She had apparently been frightened by the approach of a young man carrying a camera.

"Hi, boys," the young man said. "I'm Fred Brown. I'm a reporter for *The Hollywood News*, and I'm looking for a human interest story. I'd like to take your picture with the trunk. It's the only thing at all unusual in the sale. Just lift it up, will you? That's fine. And you — " he spoke to Bob — "stand behind it so you'll be in the picture."

Bob and Pete looked uncertain, but Jupe quickly motioned them into the pose the reporter wanted. Standing behind the trunk, Bob noticed that across the top were stenciled in faded white paint the words THE GREAT GULLIVER. The young man aimed the camera, a flashbulb went off, and the picture was taken.

"Thanks," the reporter said. "Now may I

have your names? And will you tell me why you refused thirty dollars for it? Seems like a nice profit to me."

"We're just curious," Jupiter said. "I think it's an old theatrical trunk and we want to see what's in it. We just bought it for fun, not to make a profit."

"Then you don't believe it has the Russian crown jewels in it?" Fred Brown chuckled.

"That's just talk," Pete said. "It might have old costumes in it."

"Could be," the young man agreed. "That name, The Great Gulliver, sounds very theatrical. Speaking of names, what did you say yours were?"

"We didn't say," Jupiter answered. "But here's our card. We're — uh — well, we investigate things."

He handed the reporter one of The Three Investigators' business cards, which the boys carried at all times. It said:

THE THREE INVESTIGATORS
"We Investigate Anything"
? ? ?

First Investigator .... Jupiter Jones
Second Investigator .... Peter Crenshaw
Records and Research .... Bob Andrews

"So?" The reporter raised his eyebrows. "You're investigators, eh? What do the question marks stand for?"

"That's our symbol," Jupiter told him. "The question marks stand for mysteries unsolved, riddles unanswered, puzzles of any kind. So we use it as our trademark. We investigate any kind of mystery."

"And now you're investigating an old theatrical trunk." The young man smiled and put the card in his pocket. "Thanks a lot. Maybe you'll see your picture in tonight's paper. Depends on whether the editor likes the story or not."

He raised his hand in a gesture of good-bye and turned away. Jupe picked up his end of the trunk again.

"Come on, Pete, we have to get this outside," he said. "We can't keep Hans waiting any longer."

With Bob leading the way, he and Pete lugged the trunk toward the street entrance. Pete was still grumbling.

"Why did you tell that fellow our names?" he said.

"Publicity," Jupiter said. "Every business needs publicity for people to know about it. Lately good mysteries have been scarce, and we can use some business or we'll get rusty."

10

They went through a big door, out onto the sidewalk, and down the street a few yards to where the light truck was parked. After heaving the trunk into the back, the boys climbed into the cab of the truck with Hans.

"Back home, Hans," Jupiter said. "We have made a purchase and we wish to examine it."

"Sure, Jupe," Hans agreed, getting the truck started. "You buy something, huh?"

"An old trunk," Pete said. "How're we going to open it?"

"We have lots of keys around the salvage yard," Jupiter told him. "If we're lucky one of them will work."

"Maybe we'll have to break it open," Bob suggested.

"No." Jupiter shook his head. "That would spoil it. We'll get the lock open somehow."

They rode the rest of the way in silence. When they reached The Jones Salvage Yard in Rocky Beach, Pete and Jupe handed down the trunk to Hans, who set it to one side. Mrs. Jones came out of the little cabin that served as an office.

"Mercy and goodness, what have you bought?" she asked. "Why, that trunk looks old enough to have come over on the *Mayflower*."

"Not quite, Aunt Mathilda," Jupiter said. "But it is old. We paid a dollar for it."

11

"Well, at least you didn't waste much money on it," said his aunt. "I suppose you need the bunch of keys to try to open it. They're on a nail over the desk."

Bob ran in to get the keys. Jupe began trying all that seemed the right size. After about half an hour he gave up. None of the keys would open the trunk.

"Now what'll we do?" Pete asked.

"Pry it open?" Bob suggested.

"Not yet," Jupe told them. "I believe Uncle Titus has more keys put away someplace. We'll have to wait until he comes back and ask him for them."

Jupiter's aunt came out of the office again.

"Well, boys," she said briskly, "can't waste all day. Time to get to work. First lunch, then work. You'll have to let the old trunk wait."

Reluctantly the boys went for lunch in the neat, two-story house just outside the salvage yard where Jupiter lived with his Aunt Mathilda and Uncle Titus. Then they set to work mending and repairing broken articles in the salvage yard. Titus Jones would later sell these, giving them part of the profit for spending money. This kept them well occupied until late in the afternoon, when Titus Jones and Konrad, the other yard helper, came lumbering into the yard in the big truck, bearing a load of junk Mr. Jones had bought that day.

Titus Jones, a small man with a large nose and an enormous black mustache, hopped down as lightly as a boy and embraced his wife. Then he waved a newspaper he held in his hand.

"Gather round, boys!" he called. "You're in the newspaper."

Curiously the three boys joined him and his wife, and Titus Jones spread out *The Hollywood News* to show them the first page of the second section. There, sure enough, was their picture — Jupe and Pete holding the old trunk, Bob standing behind it. It was a good picture — even the name THE GREAT GULLIVER was clear on the trunk. A headline said YOUNG SLEUTHS TO INVESTIGATE MYSTERY TRUNK. The story below it told, in a humorous manner, of Jupiter's buying the trunk and refusing to sell it for a profit, and hinted that the boys expected to find something very mysterious or valuable inside it. Of course, this last was just the reporter's imagination, thrown in to make the story more entertaining. The boys had had no idea what they'd find inside the trunk.

The story also gave their names and said their Headquarters was in The Jones Salvage Yard in Rocky Beach.

"Well, that's publicity, all right," Pete said. "It makes us sound kind of foolish, though, thinking there's something valuable in the trunk."

"That was because the auctioneer talked about the Russian crown jewels," Jupiter said. "We'll have to cut this out and add it to our scrapbook."

"Later," Mrs. Jones said firmly. "It's dinner-time now. Put the trunk away and wash up. Bob, Pete, are you going to eat with us to-night?"

Bob and Pete ate at Jupiter's home about as often as they did at their own. But this time they thought they'd better get on home, so they pedaled off on their bicycles. Jupiter pushed the old trunk out of the way around the corner of the office and went in to dinner. Mr. Jones came along behind and locked the big iron front gates of the salvage yard — fancy ornamental gates bought from an estate that burned down.

The rest of the evening was uneventful until, just as Jupiter was going up to bed, there came a soft knocking on the door. It was Hans and Konrad, who lived in a small house in the back.

"Just want to tell you, Mr. Jones," Hans said softly. "We see a light in the salvage yard, we look through the fence, somebody is fooling around in there. Maybe we all better see, huh?"

"Mercy and goodness and sweetness and light! Burglars!" Mrs. Jones gasped.

"We'll take a look, Mathilda, my dear," Mr. Jones said. "With Hans and Konrad, we can handle any burglar. We'll slip up on the intruders and catch them by surprise."

He and the two husky yard helpers began to move cautiously toward the front gates of the salvage yard. Jupiter tagged along behind. No one had suggested he come, but on the other hand, no one had said he couldn't.

Now through the cracks in the board fence surrounding the yard, they could see flickers of light from a flashlight inside. They tiptoed forward. Then — disaster! Hans tripped over something, fell heavily to the ground, and let out a surprised "Oof!"

Whoever was inside the yard heard him. Immediately they heard the sound of running feet. Two dark figures ran out through the front gate, leaped into a car parked across the street, and roared away.

Mr. Jones, Konrad, and Jupiter ran up swiftly. The front gate stood open, the lock obviously picked. The thieves were gone. But Jupiter, with a sudden suspicion, ran to where he had left the old trunk he had bought.

The mystery trunk was gone!

AN UNUSUAL
VISITOR

Bob Andrews rode his bicycle through the front gate of The Jones Salvage Yard. It was a bright sunny morning in late summer and the day promised to be warm. Pete and Jupiter were already busy in the yard. Pete was taking apart a rusty power mower, and Jupiter was putting a coat of white enamel on some iron garden chairs from which he had sanded the rust.

They looked up, dejected, as Bob parked his bike and walked over.

"Hello, Bob," Jupiter said. "Take a brush and get busy. We have a lot of these chairs to paint."

"Did you get the trunk open?" Bob burst out. "What was inside it?"

"The trunk?" Pete laughed hollowly. "What trunk are you talking about, Bob?"

"You know what trunk," Bob said, puzzled. "The trunk Jupe bought yesterday at the auction. My mom thought the picture of the three of us was pretty good. She's curious about the trunk too."

"Everybody seems to be curious about that trunk," Jupiter said, dabbing on more paint. "Too curious. We should have sold it and made a profit while we were at it."

"What do you mean?" Bob demanded.

"He means there isn't any trunk," Pete said. "Not anymore. It was stolen last night."

"Stolen!" Bob stared at him. "Who stole it?"

"We don't know," Jupiter said and then told Bob about the disturbance of the night before. "Two men ran off and got away," Jupiter finished. "And the trunk was gone. Obviously they stole it."

"Golly, I wonder why they wanted it!" Bob exclaimed. "What do you suppose was in it?"

"Maybe they were just curious too," Pete suggested. "They read the story in the paper and they came to have a look."

"I don't think so." Jupiter shook his head. "No one would steal a dollar trunk just out of curiosity. Too much risk. They must have had a good idea something valuable was in it. I'm beginning to think that trunk would have been worth investigating. Too bad we don't have it anymore."

The boys' talk was interrupted by the arrival of an expensive blue car. A tall thin man with strangely slanting eyebrows got out and came toward them.

"Ah, good morning," he said. He looked at Jupiter. "Jupiter Jones, I believe."

"Yes, sir," Jupiter said. "Can I help you? My aunt and uncle are away for a little while, but if there's anything in the salvage yard you're interested in, I can sell it to you."

"I am interested in only one thing," the tall man said. "Yesterday, according to information in the local press, you bought an old trunk. At an auction. For the large sum of one dollar. Are the facts as I state them correct?"

"Yes, sir," Jupiter answered, staring at him. Both his appearance and manner of speaking were certainly a little odd. "That's true."

"Very good," the tall man said. "To waste no more time in conversation, I wish to buy the trunk from you. I hope, I do hope you haven't sold it yet."

"Well, no sir," Jupe admitted. "We haven't sold it. But — "

18

"Then all is well," the stranger said. He waved his hand, and a number of green bills appeared between his fingers, spread out like a fan.

"Look," he said. "One hundred dollars. Ten ten-dollar bills. I offer them to you for the trunk." As Jupiter hesitated, he went on, "Surely that is enough? You cannot expect me to pay more for one old-fashioned trunk containing nothing but odds and ends, can you?"

"No, sir," Jupiter began again. "But — "

"There is no need to keep saying but!" the man snapped. "I am offering you a fair price. I want the trunk for sentimental reasons. The story in the newspaper said it had once belonged to The Great Gulliver. Is that correct?"

"Well," Jupe answered as Bob and Pete watched in puzzled interest, "that name was on it. But — "

"But again!" The tall man scowled. "But me no buts! Shakespeare said that and I say it. The fact is, The Great Gulliver was once a friend of mine. I have not seen him for some years. I fear, alas, that he is no more. Departed. Gone. To put it bluntly, dead. I should like to own his trunk for old-times' sake. Here is my card."

He snapped his fingers. The money in his hand changed to a small white card. He extended it to Jupiter, who took it. The card said *Maximilian the Mystic.* A line below that said he lived at the Sorcerers' Club, at an address in Hollywood.

"You're a magician!" Jupiter exclaimed. Maximilian the Mystic gave a slight bow.

"Once well-known," he answered. "Performances before all the crowned heads of Europe. Now in retirement, devoting myself to writing a history of magic. An occasional small exhibition of my skills for friends. But back to business."

He snapped his fingers and again the money was in his hands.

"Let us complete our transaction," he said. "I have the money. I wish the trunk. You are in business to buy and sell. It is as simple as that. You sell, I buy. Why do you hesitate?"

"Because I can't sell you the trunk!" Jupiter burst out. "That's what I've been trying to tell you."

"Can't?" The slanting eyebrows of the magician drew close together. His scowl was black. "Of course you can. Do not make me angry, boy. I still have mystic powers. Suppose — " he thrust his head toward Jupiter and his dark eyes gleamed — "suppose I snapped my fingers and made you vanish? Pouf! Like that. Into thin air. Never to return. Then you might be sorry you had made me angry."

Mr. Maximilian sounded so ominous that both Bob and Pete gulped. Even Jupe looked uneasy.

"I can't sell you the trunk," he said, "because I haven't got it. It was stolen last night."

"Stolen! Is this the truth, boy?"

"Yes, sir." Jupiter proceeded to relate, for the third time that morning, the events of the night before. Maximilian listened intently. Then he sighed.

"Alas!" he said. "I should have come the moment I read the newspaper. You have no clue to the thieves?"

"They got away before we could get close to them," Jupe said.

"Bad, very bad," the magician muttered. "To think that the trunk of The Great Gulliver should reappear so strangely, only to vanish again. I wonder why they wanted it."

"Maybe there is something valuable in it after all," Bob suggested.

"Nonsense!" Maximilian said. "The Great Gulliver never had anything valuable, poor chap. Except his magic act. There might be some of his old tricks in the trunk, but they would be valuable only to another magician, such as myself. Did I tell you The Great Gulliver was a magician? But of course you guessed it.

"He was not really great, though he called

himself that. A small man, roly-poly, with a round face and black hair. He sometimes wore Oriental robes to look like an Oriental wizard. He had one special act and I had hoped that perhaps — but no matter. The trunk is gone."

He was silent, thinking. Then he shrugged and the money between his fingers vanished.

"My trip has been for nothing," he said. "Still, there is a possibility you will get the trunk back. If you ever do, remember — Maximilian the Mystic wishes it!"

He fixed penetrating eyes on Jupiter.

"Do you understand, young man? I wish the trunk. I will pay for it if it can be recovered. You will contact me at the Sorcerers' Club. Is it agreed?"

"I don't see how we could hope to get the trunk back again," Pete said.

"Nevertheless it may happen," Maximilian insisted. "And if it does, I have first claim to it. Is that agreed, boy?"

"If we should get it back," Jupiter said, "we won't sell it to anybody else without talking to you first, Mr.. Maximilian. That's all I can promise. As Pete says, I don't see how we could possibly get the trunk again. Those thieves are probably a long ways away by now."

"I suppose so." The magician sounded depressed. "Well, we'll wait and see what happens. Don't lose my card now."

He put his hand into his pocket, seemed surprised, and brought out an egg.

"Now how in the world did that get there?" he asked. "I certainly don't want an egg in my pocket. Here, boy, catch it."

He threw the egg toward Pete, who quickly put up his hand to catch it. But in midair the egg vanished. It seemed to wink out like a light.

"Hmmm," the magician murmured, "it must have been a dodo's egg. They're extinct, you know. Well, well, I must be going. Don't forget to call me."

He strode to his car. The Three Investigators half expected something strange to happen as he went, but he simply drove out the gates and turned down the street.

"Wow!" Pete said. "That was some customer!"

"He certainly wanted that trunk badly," Jupiter added. "I wonder if it's just because he and The Great Gulliver were both magicians. Or if there's something special in that trunk that he'd like to have for himself."

They were pondering this when another car drove in through the gate. At first they thought it was Mr. Maximilian returning. Then they saw it was a smaller car, a little foreign sedan. It stopped, and out stepped a young man, whom they recognized as the reporter who had taken their picture at the auction the previous day.

"Hi, there," he said. "Remember me — Fred Brown?"

"Yes, sir," Jupiter answered. "What can we do for you?"

"I came to see if you had opened the trunk yet," the reporter told him. "I think I can get another feature story about that trunk. You see, it may have something special in it. I think it contains a talking skull!"

MYSTERY UPON MYSTERY

"A talking skull?" the boys exclaimed together. Fred Brown nodded.

"That's right. A genuine talking skull. Did you find it?"

Jupiter had to admit they hadn't found anything in the trunk because it had been stolen. Again he told the story. The reporter frowned.

"Darn!" he said. "There goes my feature! I wonder who took it? Somebody who read the story in the newspaper, I suppose."

"I suppose so, Mr. Brown," Jupiter agreed. "Maybe somebody else knew about that talking skull and wanted it. Was it a skull that really talks?"

"Call me Fred," the reporter said. "I can't tell

you if the skull really talked or not. I just know it was supposed to. You see, I began thinking about that name on the trunk — The Great Gulliver. I was sure I'd heard it before. So I looked it up in the morgue — you know what a newspaper morgue is?"

They nodded. Bob's father was a newspaperman, so they knew that a newspaper morgue is a room where old news stories, clippings, and pictures are kept on file to be used for research. It is actually a library of facts about people and events.

"Well," Fred Brown went on, "I decided to look up The Great Gulliver. Sure enough, there were several stories about him. It seems that though he wasn't very much of a magician, he had one special trick. He had a talking skull.

"A year ago Gulliver just vanished. Into thin air, like one of his tricks. Nobody knows if he died or what. But apparently he left his trunk behind at the hotel, and it came up for auction yesterday and you bought it. I figured that he probably had his magic apparatus in the trunk, including the skull, and it would make a good story."

"You say he vanished?" Bob asked.

"The whole thing is becoming quite mysterious." Jupiter frowned a bit. "A vanishing magician, a vanishing trunk, and a skull that is supposed to talk. Very mysterious indeed."

"Now wait a minute, wait a minute!" Pete protested. "I don't like the look on your face, Jupe. You're thinking of turning this into an investigation, and I don't want to investigate any talking skulls. As far as I'm concerned, such a thing doesn't exist and I don't want to learn different."

"We can't very well investigate anything now that the trunk is gone," Jupiter told him. "But I would like to know more about The Great Gulliver, Fred."

"Sure," the reporter said. He sat down on one of Jupe's unpainted iron chairs. "I'll give you the background. Gulliver was a small-time magician, but he had this skull that apparently talked. It would sit on a glass table, with no apparatus around it, and answer questions."

"Ventriloquism?" Jupiter asked. "Gulliver actually did the talking without moving his lips?"

"Well, maybe. But it would talk when Gulliver was sitting across the room from it, and sometimes even when he was out of the room. Even other magicians couldn't figure out how it was done. But eventually it got him into trouble with the police."

"How did that happen?" Bob asked.

"Well, Gulliver wasn't doing very well as a magician so he turned to fortune-telling, which is illegal. He didn't call it fortune-telling — he called himself an adviser. But he dressed up in Oriental robes and sat in a little room decorated with mystic symbols. For a fee, superstitious people could come and ask the skull questions. He even named the skull after an ancient Greek wise man — Socrates."

"And the skull answered the questions?" Bob asked.

"So it was said. Supposedly it gave some good advice too, to people with problems. But Gulliver went too far. Socrates began giving advice on the stock market and things like that, and some people lost money and complained to the police. Gulliver was charged with illegal fortune-telling and sent to jail.

"He was in jail about a year. When he got out, he gave up magic and fortune-telling and got a job as a clerk. Then one day — pouf! Like that he disappeared. There were rumors that some very tough individuals were interested in him — no one knows why. Perhaps they had some criminal scheme they wanted to involve him and Socrates in, and he disappeared to get away from them."

"But he didn't take his trunk with him." Jupiter pinched his lower lip, which always stimulated his mental machinery. "That makes it seem that either something happened to him, or he vanished on the spur of the moment."

"Good thinking," Fred said. "Perhaps he was in an accident and never identified."

"I'll bet that's why Maximilian wanted the trunk," Pete put in. "He wanted to get that skull and learn the secret for his own magic act. Maybe he really used to be Gulliver's friend, but he thought that if Gulliver was gone he might as well have Gulliver's tricks for himself."

"Maximilian?" Fred Brown asked, and Jupiter explained about the visit earlier from the tall thin magician.

"If he tried to buy the trunk, he certainly wasn't behind its theft," Fred said. "I wonder if the thieves thought they could put Socrates to work for them. Well, I don't suppose it matters. I was hoping to get a good story with a picture of you boys with the skull, and maybe you, Jupiter, dressed up in Gulliver's robes. But that's impossible, so I'd better be going. Nice to have seen you again."

Fred Brown drove away. Jupiter looked unhappy.

"It certainly would have been an interesting

mystery to investigate," he said. "I'm sorry the trunk is gone."

"Well, I'm not," Pete said. "Any trunk that has a talking skull in it can stay gone, as far as I'm concerned. I don't want any part of it. How can a skull talk, anyway?"

"That's part of the mystery," Jupiter answered. "But there's no use thinking about it because — oh, here comes Uncle Titus back now."

The big truck drove into the yard, loaded with more junk for the salvage yard. Jupiter's uncle hopped out and walked over.

"Hard at work, I see," he said to them and winked. "Good thing Mathilda isn't here. She'd find something for you to do. But you all look pretty thoughtful. Thinking about something important?"

"The truth is, we're thinking about that trunk that disappeared last night," Jupiter told him. "We've just learned something interesting about it."

"Oh, that trunk." Titus Jones chuckled. "It hasn't showed up again, then?"

"Why, no, it hasn't," Jupiter said. "I don't suppose we'll ever see it again."

"Now I wouldn't say that," Titus Jones told him. "Magician's trunk, wasn't it? Well, then, maybe we can make it come back by using magic on it."

The boys all stared at him.

"What do you mean, Uncle Titus?" Jupiter asked. "What kind of magic could bring it back?"

"Maybe this kind." Titus Jones looked mysterious. He snapped his fingers three times, turned around with his eyes closed, and chanted, "Abracadabra, a trunk we lack. Now it's time that trunk comes back.

"There," he finished, "that's a magic spell. And if that doesn't work, maybe we can get the trunk back just by using logic."

"Logic?" Jupiter was thoroughly puzzled now. His uncle was a merry type of man who enjoyed jokes. It looked as if he was having some kind of joke with them now, but Jupiter couldn't be sure.

"You like riddles and mysteries, Jupiter," Titus Jones said. "You like to solve them by being logical. Now think about what happened last night. Describe it to me."

"Well..." said Jupiter, still trying to puzzle out what his uncle was leading up to, "we all came toward the yard. Two men ran out and jumped in a car and drove away. The trunk was gone."

"So they stole it, eh?" his uncle asked.

"They must have," Jupiter said. "They picked the lock of the gate and — wait a minute!" he cried. His round face turned a little pink with both excitement and chagrin. "They were still in the salvage yard, apparently looking for the trunk, when we went after them. They ran to their car and drove off. But they didn't have the trunk when they ran out. So how could they have stolen it? If they'd already had it in their car, they wouldn't have hung around. And since they didn't carry it with them, they must not have been the thieves. There's only one conclusion. The trunk was already stolen before those two men got here!"

Mr. Jones chuckled. "Jupiter," he said, "you're smart. But sometimes it does a person good to find out he isn't as smart as he thinks is. There's another conclusion you've missed. Maybe the trunk wasn't stolen. Maybe those two men just couldn't find it."

"But I left it beside the office," Jupiter said. "Right out in plain sight. Maybe I should have locked it inside the office, but I didn't think it was valuable enough for that."

"And after you went in to get washed up for supper, and Hans and I were locking up," Titus Jones said, "I said to myself, 'That's a magician's trunk, and wouldn't it be a surprise for Jupiter if it disappeared magically! He could have some good exercise hunting for it.' So I played a little joke on you, Jupiter. I hid the trunk. Then when we surprised those would-be thieves, I thought I'd just leave it hidden until morning in case they tried again. I was going to tell you about it. But then I decided to see if you could figure things out for yourself. Stimulate your thinking machinery a little."

"You hid it?" Bob burst out. "Where, Mr. Jones?" And Pete echoed, "Where?"

"Where would be a good place to hide a trunk so it wouldn't be noticed?" Mr. Jones asked. But already Jupiter was looking all around them, at the piles of timber and old machinery and other objects that crowded the yard. The trunk could have been hidden under almost anything. But Jupiter's gaze came to rest on something over against the wall. There was a six-foot-wide roof extending from the top of the wall into the yard, and under this roof were kept the more valuable items in the salvage yard, where they would be protected from the occasional Southern California rain.

In one spot, half a dozen old trunks were lined up. They were all sturdy and in good repair. And they were all large.

"The perfect place to hide a small trunk would be in a big trunk!" Jupiter burst out. "Is that what you did, Uncle Titus?"

"You could always look and see," his uncle suggested.

Jupiter started toward the trunks. But Pete ran ahead and flung open the first trunk. It was empty. Jupiter opened the next one. It too was empty. So were the third and the fourth.

By the time they got to the fifth trunk, Bob had joined them. And as the lid went up, they all stared.

Inside the big trunk, just fitting neatly, was the mystery trunk of The Great Gulliver.

INTRODUCING
SOCRATES

"Now let's see if any of these keys Uncle Titus gave us will open the trunk," Jupiter said.

The three boys were back in Jupiter's workshop, hidden from the front of the salvage yard by piles of secondhand material. They had swiftly taken the auction trunk from its hiding place back to where they could work on it unseen.

Some customers wandered around in the front part of the salvage yard, looking for various odds and ends. Mathilda Jones was on hand to deal with them. Titus had told Jupiter he could have some time off with Bob and Pete, until Titus came back with the load of goods he was going to pick up.

As Jupiter worked on the lock, he was still feeling annoyed with himself for not suspecting that the trunk had been in the yard all along. Uncle Titus had played an embarrassing joke on him, but a good one. He should have known better than to jump to conclusions the night before. He should have at least realized the truth by morning, he reflected. He had let surface appearances deceive him completely.

"I made a mistake last night in not analyzing the facts thoroughly," he said. "It teaches you more than you'd learn from doing a thing right the first time. Uncle Titus taught me a good lesson."

Bob and Pete smiled and nodded.

"What about Mr. Maximilian?" Bob asked. "We promised to let him know if the trunk reappeared."

"We promised to let him know before we sold it to anyone else," Jupiter said. "We aren't planning on selling it, at least not now."

"I vote to sell it," Pete said. "After all, Maximilian offered us a pretty nice profit."

But the idea of owning a talking skull had gripped Jupiter's imagination.

"We can think about selling it later," he said. "I want to find out first if Socrates will really talk."

"That's what I was afraid of," Pete said with a sigh.

Jupe continued trying the keys. Finally one made the old lock turn. After unbuckling the two long leather straps that held the lid down, Jupiter lifted the lid.

They all peered in. A length of red silk cloth covered the inside of the trunk. Beneath the cloth was the top tray of the trunk, where a number of small objects were packed, some of them wrapped in different-colored silk cloths. There was a collapsible birdcage, a small crystal ball with a stand, many small red balls, several packs of playing cards, and some metal cups that fitted snugly into one another. There was not, however, a skull or any bundle big enough to contain one.

"Some of Gulliver's magic tricks," Jupiter stated. "If there's anything important, it'll be underneath, I guess."

He and Pete lifted out the top tray and set it to one side. Underneath there seemed to be mostly clothing. It was not ordinary clothing, however, for as they lifted it out, piece by piece, they saw that it consisted of several silk jackets, a long golden robe, a turban, and other Oriental-looking clothing.

It was Bob who spotted what they were looking for.

"There it is!" he said. "There at the side. Under that purple cloth. Something round. I bet it's the skull."

"I think you're right, Records," Jupiter agreed.

Jupe lifted out the round object and Bob whisked off the purple wrappings. There in Jupiter's hands sat a skull, gleaming white, that seemed to look up at him out of empty eye sockets. It was not a scary skull — somehow it even seemed friendly. It reminded the boys of the complete skeleton in the biology department at school, which everyone called Mr. Bones. They were quite used to Mr. Bones, so they weren't nervous now about the magician's skull.

"I guess that's Socrates, all right," Bob said.

"There's something under it," Jupiter said. Handing Socrates to Bob, he delved down into the trunk. He came up with a disk two inches thick and about six inches across, apparently made of ivory. Strange symbols were cut into the edge of it.

"This looks like a stand for Socrates to sit on," Jupiter said. "It has depressions that would be just right to hold him."

He put the ivory disk on a nearby table and Bob placed the skull on it. Socrates sat there with what seemed to be a grin while they all stared at him.

"He certainly looks as if he might say something," Pete commented. "But if he does, I'm going to find business someplace else."

"Probably only Gulliver could make him speak," Jupiter suggested. "My theory is that he has some kind of mechanism inside."

He picked Socrates up and peered at him closely.

"Not a sign," Jupiter muttered. "If there was anything inside him I'm sure I could spot it. There would be some evidence, and there isn't — nothing at all. It's very baffling."

He put Socrates back on his ivory stand.

"Socrates, if you can really talk, say something," he ordered.

His only answer was silence.

"Well, he doesn't seem to be in a talking mood," Jupiter said at last. "Let's see what else is in the trunk."

He and Bob and Pete began pulling out more Oriental costumes. Then they found a magician's wand, and several short curved swords. They were examining these, their backs to Socrates, when a muffled sneeze sounded behind them.

They whirled around. No one was there. No one, that is, but the skull.

Socrates had sneezed!

STRANGE TALK
IN THE DARK

The boys looked at each other with round eyes.

"He sneezed!" Pete said. "That's the next thing to talking. If a skull can sneeze it can probably recite the Gettysburg Address!"

"Hmmm." Jupiter scowled. "You're sure it wasn't you who sneezed, Bob?"

"It wasn't any of us," Bob said. "I distinctly heard the sneeze behind us."

"Peculiar," Jupiter muttered. "If it was some trick of The Great Gulliver's that made the skull talk or make sounds, I could understand it. But Gulliver isn't here. He may be dead. I just don't see how a skull could sneeze all by itself. Let's examine it again."

41

He picked up the skull and turned it over and over in his hands, studying it intently. He even held it up to the sunshine to get a better light. But there was absolutely no sign that Socrates had been tampered with in any way.

"No wires or anything," Jupiter said. "This is really quite mysterious."

"I'll buy a double helping of that!" Pete exclaimed.

"But *why* should a skull sneeze?" Bob demanded. "There's no reason for it to."

"I don't know why, and I don't know how," Jupiter said. "But it should make a very nice mystery for us to investigate. It's the kind of mystery that Alfred Hitchcock would be willing to introduce for us, I bet."

He was speaking of the famous motion-picture producer who had steered them to several of their most mystifying cases and who took a keen interest in their work.

"Now wait a minute!" Pete cried. "Last night two men tried to steal this trunk. Today we open it and find a sneezing skull in it. The next thing you know — "

He was interrupted by Mathilda Jones's powerful voice.

"Jupiter! Boys! I know you're back there! Come a-running. There's work to be done!"

"Oh, oh!" Bob said. "Your aunt wants us."

"And that's her 'don't-make-me-wait' voice," Pete added as Mathilda Jones's voice came again, calling to Jupiter. "We'd better get out front."

"Yes, indeed," Jupiter said hastily. He put Socrates back in the trunk and locked it and then they all trotted to the front section of the salvage yard. Mrs. Jones was waiting, her hands on her hips.

"There you are!" she said. "It's about time. Your Uncle Titus and Hans and Konrad have unloaded all that stuff he bought, and I'd like you boys to sort it out and stack it."

The three boys looked at the pile of second-hand goods in front of the office and sighed. It would take a long time to put it all away neatly, but one thing Mrs. Jones insisted on was neatness. The Jones Salvage Yard was a junkyard, but a very high class and unusual one, and she would tolerate no unnecessary untidiness.

The boys set to work, pausing only for the lunch that Mrs. Jones brought out to them. Just when they seemed almost through, Titus Jones arrived with another truckload of furniture and odds and ends he had bought from an apartment house going out of business.

So they were busy all afternoon, and though Jupiter itched to get back to the trunk and its strange contents, he had no chance. Finally Bob and Pete had to start for home. Pete agreed to meet Jupe back at the yard the next morning. Bob would come by later, as he had to work at his part-time job in the local library in the morning.

Jupiter ate a hearty dinner and then was too drowsy to think much about the mystery of the trunk of the missing magician and the supposedly talking skull. However, it did occur to him that if thieves had tried to steal the trunk once, they might try again.

He went out and let himself into the salvage yard, and got Socrates and his ivory stand from the trunk. Putting everything else back in, he locked the trunk and hid it behind the printing press with some old canvas over it. It should be safe there, he decided, but he was determined to take no chance with Socrates. He took the skull back to the house with him.

As he entered the living room with Socrates, his aunt glanced up and gave a slight scream.

"Stars and comets, Jupiter!" she exclaimed. "What is that awful thing you're carrying?"

"It's just Socrates," Jupiter told her. "He's supposed to be able to talk."

"Be able to talk, eh?" Titus Jones looked up from his newspaper and chuckled. "What does he say, my boy? He has a rather intelligent appearance."

44

"He hasn't said anything yet," Jupiter admitted. "I'm hoping he will, though. But I don't really expect him to."

"Well, he'd better not talk to me or I'll give him a piece of my mind!" Mathilda Jones said. "The idea! Get him out of my sight, Jupiter. I don't want to look at him."

Jupiter took Socrates up to his bedroom and set him on his ivory base on the bureau. Then he went back downstairs to watch television.

By the time he went to bed he had decided that Socrates couldn't possibly talk. The answer must be that The Great Gulliver, his owner, had been a very gifted ventriloquist.

He had almost fallen asleep when a soft whistle roused him. It came again, and it sounded as if it were right in the room with him.

Suddenly wide awake, Jupiter sat upright in bed.

"Who's that? Is that you, Uncle Titus?" he asked, thinking for a moment that his uncle might be playing another joke.

"It is I," came a soft, rather high-pitched voice from the darkness in the direction of his bureau. "Socrates."

"Socrates?" Jupiter gulped.

"The time has come...to speak. Do not turn on...the light. Just listen and...do not be frightened. Do you...understand?"

45

The words came as if with difficulty. Jupiter stared through the darkness to where Socrates was but could see nothing.

"Well — all right." He spoke the words with a slight gulp.

"Good," said the voice. "You must go...to-morrow...to 311 King Street. The password ...is Socrates. Do you...understand?"

"Yes," said Jupiter, more boldly. "But what is this all about? Who is talking to me?"

"I...Socrates." The whispering voice trailed away. Jupiter reached out and switched on the bedside lamp. He stared across at Socrates. The skull seemed to grin back, quite silent now.

Socrates couldn't have been speaking to him! But — the voice had been in his room. It hadn't come from the window.

At the thought of the window, Jupiter turned to it. He peered out. The yard outside was quite open, and there was no one in sight anywhere.

Extremely baffled, Jupiter got back into bed.

The message had been for him to go to 311 King Street the next day. Maybe he shouldn't — but he knew he would. The mystery was getting more perplexing.

And if there was anything Jupiter couldn't resist, it was a good mystery.

A MYSTERIOUS
MESSAGE

"You're sure you don't want me to come in with you, Jupe?" Pete asked.

Sitting in the front seat of the light truck, which Hans had driven into Los Angeles for them, Pete and Jupiter were staring at the dingy building which stood at 311 King Street. A faded sign on the porch said ROOMS. Underneath was a smaller sign that said *No Vacancies*.

The neighborhood was rundown. There were other rooming houses and some stores, and everything needed paint and repair. The few people on the street were quite old. It seemed to be a street where elderly people with small incomes lived.

"I don't think so, Second," Jupiter answered. "You wait here for me in the truck with Hans. I don't think there's any danger."

Pete swallowed hard. "You say the skull *told* you to come here?" he asked. "Just like that? Sitting on your bureau it talked to you in the dark?"

"Either that or I had a very remarkable dream," Jupiter told him. "But I wasn't asleep so I don't think I was dreaming. I'll go in and see what it's all about. If I'm not out in twenty minutes, you and Hans come in after me."

"Well, if you say so," Pete agreed. "But there's a lot about this business I don't like."

"If there's any danger," Jupiter said, "I'll yell as loudly as I can for help."

"Be careful, Jupe," said Hans, his big round face showing concern. "And if you need help, we come quick!"

He flexed his powerful arm to show that, if necessary, he'd break down doors to rescue Jupiter. The First Investigator nodded.

"I'll count on both of you," he said as he got out of the truck.

Jupe went up the walk to a small front porch, climbed some steps, and pushed the doorbell. He waited for what seemed like a long time before he heard a step inside.

The door opened. A heavyset man with

swarthy features and a mustache looked at him.

"Yes?" he asked. "What do you want, boy? No rooms for rent. All full."

His accent was slightly foreign and Jupiter could not place it. He put on his stupid look, which he sometimes adopted when he wanted adults to think he was just a dumb, pudgy boy. "I'm looking for Mr. Socrates," he said, using the password.

"Hah!" For a long moment the man stared at him. Then he stepped back. "You come in. Maybe he here, maybe he not. All depends. Lonzo will ask."

Jupiter stepped inside and blinked his eyes in the dim light. The hall was dusty and small. Opening off it was a large room where several other men sat reading newspapers or playing checkers. All had swarthy features, very black hair, and muscular builds. All looked up and stared at Jupiter with expressionless faces.

Jupiter waited. Finally the man with the mustache came back from a room at the far end of the hall.

"You come," he said. "Zelda will see you."

He led Jupiter down the hall into the room, then left and closed the door behind him. Jupiter blinked his eyes. The room was bright and sunny, and after the dark hall it took him a moment to see the old woman sitting in a big rocking chair. She was knitting something while looking at him keenly through old-fashioned spectacles.

She wore a bright red-and-yellow robe and had large gold rings in her ears. As she peered up at him, Jupiter suddenly realized she was a Gypsy. Her first words confirmed this.

"I am Zelda, the Gypsy," she said in a soft, husky voice. "What does the young man wish? To have his fortune told?"

"No, ma'am," Jupiter said politely. "Mr. Socrates told me to come here."

"Ah, Mr. Socrates," the old Gypsy woman said. "But Mr. Socrates is dead."

Thinking of the skull, Jupiter had to admit that Socrates was dead all right.

"But still he spoke to you," Zelda murmured. "Strange, very strange. Sit down, young man. There, at that table. I shall consult the crystal."

Jupiter sat down at a small table made of rich wood inlaid with ivory in strange designs. Zelda rose and seated herself opposite him. From beneath the table she picked up a small box, out of which she took a crystal ball. She put the ball in the center of the table.

"Silence!" she hissed. "Say nothing. Do not disturb the crystal."

Jupiter nodded. The old Gypsy placed her

hands lightly on the table and leaned forward to stare into the shiny crystal ball. She was very still. Indeed, she seemed to have stopped breathing. Long moments passed. At last she spoke.

"I see a trunk," she murmured. "I see men — many men who wish the trunk. I see another man. He is afraid. His name begins with B — no, with G. He is afraid and he wishes help. He is asking you to help him. The crystal clears! I see money — much money. Many men want it. But it is hidden. It is behind a cloud, it vanishes, no one knows where it goes.

"The crystal is clouding. The man whose name begins with G is gone. He has vanished from the world of men. He is dead, yet he lives. I can see no more."

The old Gypsy woman, who had been leaning forward to stare intently into the crystal ball, straightened with a sigh.

"To read the crystal takes much effort," she said. "For today I can do no more. Did my vision have meaning to you, young man?"

Jupiter scowled in puzzlement.

"Part of it did," he said. "About the trunk. I have a trunk that people seem to want. And G could stand for Gulliver. The Great Gulliver, the magician, that is."

"The Great Gulliver," the Gypsy murmured. "To be sure. He was a friend of the Gypsies. But he has disappeared."

"You said he has vanished from the world of men," Jupiter told her. "That he is dead, yet he lives. I don't understand that part at all. What does it mean?"

"I cannot say." The Gypsy shook her head. "But the crystal does not lie. We Gypsies would like to find Gulliver and bring him back, for he was our friend. Perhaps you can help. You are clever, and though you are a boy, your eye is keen. You might see things that sometimes men do not see."

"I don't know how I could help," Jupiter objected. "I don't know anything about Gulliver. And I certainly haven't heard anything about any money. All I did was buy Gulliver's trunk at an auction. It had Socrates, his talking skull, in it. Socrates told me to come here. That's all I know."

"A long journey starts with a single step," the Gypsy said. "Leave now and wait. Perhaps you will learn more. Keep the trunk safe. If Socrates speaks, listen well. Good-bye."

Jupiter rose, more puzzled than ever, and left. Lonzo, the Gypsy with the mustache, showed him out.

Pete and Hans were waiting in the truck; Pete was looking at his wristwatch.

"Golly, Jupe, we were just about to come in after you," he said as Jupiter climbed into the cab of the truck. "I'm glad you're all right. What happened?"

"I'm not sure," Jupiter said as Hans started the truck and they rolled off down the street. "I mean, I know what happened, but I don't know what it all meant."

He related the events of the past few minutes to Pete, who whistled at the story.

"That's certainly mixed up," he said. "Gulliver, and money that's hidden, and Gulliver is dead but he lives. I don't get it."

"I don't either," Jupiter said. "It's very perplexing."

"Say!" Pete exclaimed. "Do you suppose there's a lot of money hidden in Gulliver's trunk? We didn't really search it too well after we found Socrates. If there's money in it, that would explain why everybody wants to get ahold of the trunk."

"I was just thinking of that too," Jupe admitted. "Maybe it isn't Socrates at all that these people are after. We'll have another look in the trunk when we get back.... What is it, Hans? Why are you speeding up?"

"Somebody follows us," Hans muttered, accelerating still more so that they bounced and rattled along at a high speed. "A black car with two men in it is behind us for blocks."

Pete and Jupiter peered back through the rear window. Behind them was indeed a black car, now trying to overtake them. However the road was empty and Hans kept the truck in the middle of it so that the black car could not pass.

In this fashion they raced along for half a mile, then saw a freeway ahead of them. Los Angeles has many freeways — roads from four to eight lanes wide that carry traffic through the crowded city without intersections or stoplights. Some are elevated above the ordinary streets, and this was one of them.

"I get on the freeway!" Hans muttered. "They do not try to stop us there. Too much traffic."

Hans turned into the entrance road leading up to the freeway, hardly slackening speed. The truck leaned far over, then in a moment emerged on the broad freeway, where many cars sped along in both directions.

The car behind them did not try to follow. The driver must have realized that he could not stop them — if that was his plan — in the midst of so much traffic, and on a roadway where stopping was forbidden. The black car went on beneath the freeway and vanished.

"We lost them OK," Hans said. "I like to get my hands on them, bang their heads together. Where to now, Jupe?"

"Back home, Hans," Jupiter said. "What is it, Pete? What are you scowling about?"

"I don't like any of this," Pete said. "A skull that talks to you in the night. People trying to steal the trunk, and then following us. It makes me nervous. I say let's forget the whole business."

"I don't think we can forget it," Jupiter said thoughtfully. "It looks as if we have a mystery on our hands that we're going to have to solve whether we want to or not."

GOOD-BYE TO SOCRATES

When they arrived back at The Jones Salvage Yard, Mathilda Jones had some jobs for Jupe to do. Pete pitched in to help and they were kept busy until after lunch. About that time Bob arrived, having finished his morning's work at the local library. All three boys made their way back to the workshop where the old-fashioned trunk still sat, beneath the old canvas Jupiter had thrown over it.

After telling Bob about the events of the morning, Jupiter said, "According to the Gypsy, Zelda, some money apparently disappeared in some way, and that seems to be connected up with The Great Gulliver's disappearance."

"Maybe he took the money and went to Europe, or something," Bob suggested.

"No." Jupiter shook his head. "Zelda said he needed help, that he had vanished from the world of men, was dead, yet lived, and she and the other Gypsies would like to help him return. That's all very puzzling, but what I deduce is that Gulliver didn't vanish *with* the money, but *because* of the money."

"Maybe he had the money hidden in the trunk," Pete suggested, "and some tough characters were after it. Remember, Fred Brown mentioned that some tough eggs were interested in him just before he disappeared. Maybe he hid from them."

"But why would he leave the money in the trunk?" Jupiter asked. "Still, maybe he did, so the first thing to do is look thoroughly."

But half an hour later, when they had totally unpacked the trunk and had inspected everything in it carefully, they had found no sign of money or anything else valuable.

"That's that," Pete said. "Nothing."

"Money in big bills," Jupiter said, "could be hidden under the lining of the trunk and not be noticed. Look, down there in the corner there's a slight tear in the lining."

"You think it could be hidden there?" Bob

asked. "It's not nearly a big enough bump." He reached down and thrust a finger through the tear in the lining.

"There is, there's something here!" he cried excitedly. "Paper! Maybe it's money!"

Carefully he pulled out the paper he had touched and held it up.

"Not money," he said. "Just an old letter."

"Hmm," Jupiter murmured. "Let me inspect it. . . . It's addressed to Gulliver at a hotel and it's postmarked about a year ago. So he got it just about the time he disappeared. After he got it, he cut the lining of his trunk and hid the letter. That means he considered it important."

"Maybe it's a clue to the money Zelda mentioned," Bob said. "It may have a map or something in it."

He and Pete crowded close as Jupiter pulled a single sheet from the envelope. On it was written a short note. It said:

State Prison Hospital
July 17

Dear Gulliver:
Just a few words from your old pal and cellmate, Spike Neely. I'm in the hospital, and it looks like I haven't got much longer.

*I may last five days, or three weeks, or even
two months, the doctors aren't sure. But in any
case, it's time to say good-bye.*

*If you're ever in Chicago, look up my cousin
Danny Street. Tell him hello for me. Wish I
could say more, but this is all I can manage.*

*Your friend,
Spike*

"It's just a letter," Pete said, "from somebody
Gulliver knew when he was in jail for fortune-
telling, I guess. It doesn't mean anything."

"Maybe it does and maybe it doesn't," Jupiter disagreed.

"If it doesn't mean anything, why did Gulliver hide it?" Bob asked.

"That's exactly the point," Jupiter said.
"Why did he hide it? It looks as if he considered
it important, somehow."

Pete scratched his head. "Well, it certainly
doesn't say anything about any money."

"This Spike Neely was in the prison hospital
when he wrote it," Bob said. "I think that let-
ters from prisoners are always read by the authorities before they're mailed. So Spike
couldn't say anything about any money without
letting the prison authorities in on it."

"Unless somehow he did it secretly," Jupiter suggested.

"You mean a message in invisible ink, something like that?" Pete asked.

"It's a possibility. I suggest we take this letter into Headquarters and analyze it."

Jupiter went over to the iron grillwork that seemed to be leaning against the back of the printing press they had rebuilt some time ago. When moved aside, the grillwork revealed the opening of Tunnel Two, their main entrance into Headquarters. Tunnel Two was a length of large iron pipe about two feet in diameter, ridged the way pipes used in culverts are. It went, partly underground, beneath a pile of rather worthless junk until it came up underneath Headquarters, which was a mobile home trailer hidden from sight in the midst of the junk.

Jupiter went first, then Bob, then Pete, scrambling on hands and knees through Tunnel Two, which was padded with old rugs so the corrugations in the pipe would not bruise their knees. They pushed up the trapdoor at the other end and clambered out into the tiny office of Headquarters.

The three boys had built a tiny laboratory in the old trailer, complete with microscope and other necessary items. There was only room for one at a time in the lab, so Jupiter took the letter in while Pete and Bob watched from the narrow door. First Jupe put the letter under a microscope and went over it inch by inch.

"Nothing," he said. "Now I'll test for the most common kind of invisible ink."

He reached for a jar of acid and poured some into a glass beaker. He held the letter above the beaker in the acid fumes, moving it back and forth. Nothing happened.

"As I expected," he said. "Logic says that someone in a prison hospital wouldn't be able to get hold of invisible ink, anyway. He just might be able to get a lemon, though, and lemon juice is a very simple kind of invisible ink. When you write with it, the writing can't be seen, but if the paper is heated, the words written in lemon juice will appear. Let's try that."

He lit a small gas burner. Then, holding the letter by the corners, he moved it back and forth over the flame.

"Again, no results," he said after a few moments. "Let me have the envelope to test."

However, all tests on the envelope were also negative. Jupiter looked disappointed.

"It seems to be just an ordinary letter, after all," he said. "Yet, after Gulliver received it, he hid it. Why did he do that?"

"Maybe he thought there was a clue in it, but

he couldn't find it," Bob suggested. "Listen, suppose when he was in prison, this Spike Neely told him something about some hidden money, but not where it was. He could have said that because Gulliver was his friend, if anything ever happened to him he'd let Gulliver in on the secret.

"Then Gulliver gets this letter from the prison hospital. Spike is dying. Gulliver thinks Spike may have sent him a clue to where the money is, but he can't find it, so he hides the letter, planning to study it some more.

"Some other criminals who knew Spike in prison learn somehow that he wrote to Gulliver. They suspect he told Gulliver the secret. So they come around to see Gulliver. Gulliver gets very frightened. He doesn't go to the police because he doesn't know anything he can tell them. But he's afraid the crooks think he knows where the money is, and might even torture him to make him talk. So — he disappears. How does that sound?"

"Very well reasoned, Bob," Jupiter said. "I think it may be what happened.

"However, we have studied the letter and can't find any clue to a secret message. So I deduce that Spike Neely didn't send any such message. He didn't try because he knew the letter would be read first by the police."

"Just the same, somebody thinks there's a clue in that trunk," Pete stated. "They want the trunk because of the clue they expect to find. If we don't want trouble with some tough characters who will probably keep trying to get the trunk, we'd better get rid of it right away."

"Pete has something there," Bob said. "We can't solve the mystery because we haven't any clue. If we want to avoid trouble, we'd better get rid of the trunk. It doesn't mean anything to us, after all."

"Maximilian the Mystic wants us to sell it to him," Pete put in. "I vote we put Socrates back in the trunk and let Mr. Maximilian have the whole shooting match. Get it off our hands. It's too dangerous to keep around. How about it, Jupe?"

"Mmmm." Jupiter pinched his lip. "Zelda seemed to think we could help somehow, but it certainly doesn't look like it. As you say, we haven't found a clue. Two men followed us this morning when we left Zelda's house and I don't like that very much either.

"All right, we'll telephone Mr. Maximilian, since he wants the trunk so badly. We'll repack it and put Socrates back in. But we'll have to warn him about other people wanting the trunk, so he'll know. And I won't charge him a hundred dollars — just the dollar I paid for it."

"It would be awfully nice to have a hundred dollars," Pete said.

"It wouldn't be fair, if the trunk is dangerous," Jupiter said. "I'll call him in a minute. First I want to photograph this letter in case I get any new ideas."

Jupiter made several photographs of both the letter and the envelope. Then he phoned Maximilian the Mystic, who said he'd be right over for the trunk. After that they went outside and slid the letter back behind the torn lining, then repacked the trunk carefully. Finally Jupiter went to get Socrates from his room.

He reached his room just in time to find Aunt Mathilda staring with a look of horror at the skull on the bureau.

"Jupiter Jones!" she said. "That — that thing..."

Speechless, she pointed at the skull.

"Yes, Aunt Mathilda?" Jupiter asked.

"That awful thing!" the large woman exploded. "You know what it just did? It said 'boo!' to me!"

"Socrates said 'boo' to you?" Jupiter asked.

"It certainly did! I just came in here to clean your room and I said to it, 'You ugly thing, I

64

don't know where Jupiter got you, but I can tell you one thing. You're not staying in my house and that's final. I won't have it!'

"And then — then — " her voice faltered again — "it said 'boo!' just as plainly as anything. 'Boo!' I heard it as clearly as I hear you."

"It's supposed to be a talking skull," Jupiter said, suppressing a smile. "It used to belong to a magician. If it said 'boo' it was probably playing a joke on you."

"A joke? Is that what you call a joke? Having a nasty old skull grin at a person and say 'boo'? I don't care if it's a talking skull or a talking horse, I want it out of here immediately. And that's final!"

"Very well, Aunt Mathilda," Jupiter agreed. "I'll get rid of it. I was already planning to."

"Be sure you do."

In a thoughtful mood, Jupiter made his way back to the salvage yard with Socrates and the ivory base. He told Pete and Bob what had happened to his aunt.

"It's very puzzling," he concluded. "I have to admit I'm utterly baffled. Why should Socrates say 'boo' to Aunt Mathilda?"

"Maybe he has a sense of humor," Pete said. "Let's get him packed."

"After this new development," Jupiter said,

"maybe we ought to keep Socrates and the trunk for a while. Perhaps he's ready to talk some more."

"Oh, no!" Pete said, grabbing Socrates, wrapping him up, and stowing him in the old trunk. "Your aunt says you have to get rid of him, and we'd agreed to get rid of him. We also agreed to let Mr. Maximilian have him and we can't go back on our word now. I'm not in any mood to hear talk coming from a skull. Some mysteries I don't want to solve."

He closed the lid and snapped the lock shut. Just as Jupiter was trying to think of an argument, they heard Hans calling.

"Jupe! Hey, Jupe! Somebody here to see you."

"I bet that's Mr. Maximilian," Bob said as he and the others started toward the front of the salvage yard.

It was indeed the tall thin magician, standing waiting for them, ignoring the other customers wandering around and the piles of interesting junk.

"Well, boy," he exclaimed, peering at Jupiter. "So Gulliver's trunk turned up, did it?"

"Yes, sir," Jupiter answered. "And you can have it if you really want it."

"Of course I want it! Didn't I say so? Here's

66

the money — one hundred dollars."

"I'm not going to charge you a hundred dollars for it," Jupiter said. "I paid a dollar for it and you can have it for a dollar."

"Humph!" the man snorted. "Why are you being so generous, may I ask? Have you taken something valuable from it?"

"No, sir, the trunk is just the way it was when we got it. But there's a mystery connected with it, and somebody seems to want it very much. It may be dangerous to own it. I'm not sure we shouldn't turn it over to the police."

"Nonsense, boy! I shall not worry about any danger. I can take care of myself. I made the first bid for the trunk and now I demand you sell it to me. Here's your dollar."

He stretched out a long arm, snapped his fingers, and apparently took a silver dollar from Jupe's ear.

"Now the trunk is mine," he said. "Pray produce it."

"Bob, will you and Pete bring the trunk?" Jupiter asked.

"You bet we will!" said Pete. In less than a minute he and Bob brought out the trunk. The magician directed the boys to put it on the back seat of his blue sedan, parked near the gate. They were all so intent on their business that they failed to notice two men covertly watching them. Maximilian got in behind the wheel.

"Next time I give a performance," he said, "I'll send you tickets. Until then, good-bye."

The car vanished out the gate. Pete gave a sigh of relief.

"Well, there goes Socrates," he said. "I bet Mr. Maximilian hopes he can learn the secret of how it talks and use it in his magic act. He's welcome to it. We've seen the last of that skull and that trunk and I'm glad of it."

He wouldn't have sounded so happy if he'd known how wrong he was.

"THEY'VE FLOWN
THE COOP!"

The rest of the day passed without anything special happening. Bob went home early to see his father. Mr. Andrews, a feature writer for a big Los Angeles newspaper, was often away in the evening, but tonight he would be home.

"Well, Bob," his father remarked during dinner, "I saw your picture in the Hollywood paper, with the story about your friend Jupiter buying an old trunk at auction. Did you find anything interesting in it?"

"We found a skull that was supposed to be able to talk," Bob answered. "Its name is Socrates."

"A talking skull named Socrates!" his mother

exclaimed. "Good gracious, what an idea! I hope it didn't talk to you."

"No, Mom, it didn't talk to me," Bob said. He thought of mentioning that it had talked to Jupiter but decided against it. Especially as his father immediately remarked, with a smile, "Some simple trick of that magician it was supposed to have belonged to, of course — what was his name? Alexander?"

"Gulliver," Bob corrected. "The Great Gulliver."

"I imagine the man was a good ventriloquist," Mr. Andrews said. "What is Jupiter doing with it? Not keeping it, I hope."

"No, he sold it," Bob said. "To another magician who said he used to know Mr. Gulliver. A man who calls himself Maximilian the Mystic."

"Maximilian the Mystic?" his father frowned. "We had a short news flash at the paper just before I left. He was hurt in a car accident this afternoon."

Maximilian hurt in a car accident? Bob wondered if the talking skull had brought him bad luck. Then his father interrupted his thoughts.

"Say, how would you like to go sailing next Sunday?" he asked. "A friend of mine has invited us all to spend the day on his boat sailing out around Catalina Island."

"That would be great!" Bob said enthusiastically. He forgot about Maximilian's accident. He did not even remember it the next morning when he joined Pete and Jupiter at The Jones Salvage Yard.

The three boys set to work taking apart a secondhand washing machine Titus Jones had bought. By using some parts from another machine, they were able to put it in perfect working order. They had just finished the repair job when a Rocky Beach police car drove into the yard. They looked up with surprise as the heavyset figure of Police Chief Reynolds got out and walked over toward them.

"Hello, boys," he said. He looked very serious. "I have some questions to ask you."

"Questions, sir?" Jupiter asked, blinking.

"Yes. About a trunk you sold yesterday to a man who calls himself Maximilian the Mystic. He had an accident as he was driving home. His car was smashed up and he was badly hurt. He's in the hospital now. At first we thought it was an ordinary accident — he was unconscious and couldn't talk.

"But this morning he woke up and told us that another car, with two men in it, had forced him off the road. He told us about the trunk too. Apparently the two men stole the trunk, for it certainly wasn't in his wrecked car when we had it towed to a garage."

"Then apparently the two men deliberately wrecked Mr. Maximilian's car in order to get the trunk!" Jupiter exclaimed.

"Exactly what we figured out," agreed Chief Reynolds. "Maximilian couldn't talk much — the doctor wouldn't let him. He said he bought the trunk from you, Jupiter, and then the doctor said he'd talked enough. So I've come to find out what was in the trunk that would make someone want to steal it."

"Well," Jupiter told him as Pete and Bob listened intently, "there was mostly clothing in it. There was some magical apparatus. The main thing in it was an old skull that was supposed to be able to talk."

"A skull able to talk!" Chief Reynolds exploded. "That sounds crazy! Skulls can't talk!"

"No, sir," Jupiter agreed. "But this one used to belong to another magician named The Great Gulliver and — " He proceeded to tell Chief Reynolds the whole story of how they had bought the trunk at auction, what they had learned about Gulliver, how he had spent some time in jail, then had disappeared after being released.

Chief Reynolds listened, frowning and chewing his lip.

"That's certainly a mixed-up story," he said when Jupiter had finished. "You must have imagined it when you thought you heard the skull talk to you in your room the other night. Maybe it was a dream."

"I thought of that, sir. But when I went to the address it gave me, I found the Gypsy woman, Zelda, who seemed to know about Gulliver. She said he was no longer in the world of men."

Chief Reynolds sighed and mopped his forehead.

"And she spouted this stuff about hidden money that she claimed to see in the crystal, eh?" he muttered. "Well, it's certainly strange. Now about this letter you found in the trunk and put back. You say you took photographs of it. I'd like to have those photographs."

"Yes, sir," Jupiter said. "I'll get them."

He hurried back to the workshop section, slid into Tunnel Two, and was soon inside Headquarters. Early that morning he had developed the film he had taken the day before and hung up the prints to dry. He only had one set of prints, but he could make more if he needed them.

He put the dry prints in an envelope and a moment later was back, handing them to Chief Reynolds. The Chief glanced at the photographs and shook his head.

"Don't suppose they'll mean anything to me," he grumbled. "But I'll study them. Next thing I want to do, though, is talk to that Gypsy woman, Zelda. Suppose you drive down there with me now, Jupiter, and we'll see what she has to say. I have a hunch she knows more than she let on."

Bob and Pete hoped he would invite them too, but he didn't. Telling them to carry on while he was gone, Jupiter climbed into the official car with Chief Reynolds, and the policeman driver started for Los Angeles.

"This is just an unofficial visit," the Chief said to Jupiter as they sped along. "I suppose she'll clam up and not say anything. Gypsies are very closemouthed. But we'll try. I could ask the Los Angeles police for cooperation, but so far I haven't anything to go on. Zelda didn't tell your fortune, so she hasn't broken any law that I know of.

"When I get back to my office, one thing I will do, though, is start some inquiries into the background of this Spike Neely who wrote the letter to Gulliver. Let's see if we can learn what's behind all this. Certainly has to be some good reason why a couple of thugs would force a car off the road just to steal a trunk. They must have been watching the salvage yard. Must have seen you put the trunk in Maximilian's car and followed him."

Jupiter said nothing, for at this point he had

no new ideas and had to admit that he was completely puzzled by the whole affair.

The police car drove swiftly, and soon they were in front of the rundown building where Jupe had called on Zelda. Chief Reynolds led the way up the walk to the small porch and rang the bell vigorously.

They waited. There was no answer. Chief Reynolds started to look rather grim. Then an old woman sweeping down the steps of the next house called to them.

"If you're looking for those Gypsies," she said, "they're gone."

"Gone!" the Chief exclaimed. "Where'd they go?"

"Who knows where Gypsies go?" The old woman cackled. "They drove away bag and baggage in some old cars early this morning. Didn't say a word to anybody. Just cleared out."

"Thunder!" Chief Reynolds growled. "There goes our only lead. They've flown the coop!"

WARNING FROM CHIEF REYNOLDS

"The meeting will come to order," Jupiter said.

Bob Andrews and Pete Crenshaw settled themselves in their chairs. Jupiter rapped a pencil on the wooden desk in front of him in the tiny office in Headquarters.

"The Three Investigators will now discuss future projects," he said. "The meeting is open for anyone to make suggestions." When neither Bob nor Pete said anything, he added, "We all have a day off today. How shall we spend it?"

Two days had passed since the visit from Chief Reynolds. They had been quiet days, in which the three boys had put in a good many hours repairing and rebuilding secondhand items in the salvage yard. No one had come in with a mystery to be solved, rather to Bob's and Pete's relief. They were glad to have things quiet for a change. They were especially glad to have the curious problem of the talking skull and the mystery trunk off their hands.

"I move we go scuba diving today," Pete said. "It's a swell day for it and we haven't done any diving lately. We'll get rusty."

"I second the motion," Bob chimed in. "It's a hot day and the water will feel good."

At that moment the telephone rang.

They all jumped slightly and looked at it. The telephone, which they paid for out of their earnings in the salvage yard, was listed in Jupiter's name. Only a few people knew that it was The Three Investigators' official phone. It did not ring often, but when it did, the call was usually important.

The phone rang again, and Jupiter picked it up.

"Hello," he said. "The Three Investigators, Jupiter Jones speaking."

"Hello, Jupiter," answered Police Chief Reynolds. They could all hear him over the loudspeaker arrangement Jupiter had rigged up. "I called your house and your aunt told me to try this number."

"Yes, Chief?" Jupiter answered alertly.

"I told you I was going to start some inquiries," the Chief said. "You know, about that letter you photographed, and Spike Neely and The Great Gulliver. Well, I've had some answers. I'm not sure what it all means, but I'd like to talk to you some more. Can you come down to my office?"

"Yes, sir!" Jupiter said with a trace of excitement. "Right now, Chief Reynolds?"

"As good a time as any," the Chief replied. "I'm not busy this morning."

"We'll be there in twenty minutes," Jupiter told him and hung up. "Well," he said to the other two, "that takes care of our plans for this morning, anyway. Chief Reynolds has some new information."

"Oh, no!" Pete groaned. "We told him everything we knew. Anyway, you did. As far as I'm concerned, that whole business of the trunk and the skull is closed. Finished. Washed up. Out of our hands. Done with."

"Well, of course, if you don't want to come with me, I can probably handle it by myself," Jupiter said.

Bob grinned. Pete's face was a study in conflicting emotions. He didn't want to be left out of anything, no matter how much he protested.

"Oh, we'll come with you," Pete said. "The Three Investigators stick together. Maybe it won't take long and we can still go scuba diving."

"In that case, the meeting is adjourned," Jupiter stated. "Let's go."

Leaving word with Titus Jones that they would be gone for a while, they bicycled into Rocky Beach. The Jones Salvage Yard was situated on the outskirts of the small city, but it did not take long to reach the center of the town where police headquarters was located.

They parked their bikes and entered, to be greeted by the officer in charge behind the big desk.

"Go right in," they were told. "The Chief is waiting for you."

They went down a short hall to a door marked *Chief of Police*, knocked, and entered. Chief Reynolds was seated behind his desk, puffing thoughtfully on a cigar. He waved them to chairs.

"Sit down, boys," he said. They sat and waited expectantly. The Chief took another puff on the cigar before he spoke.

"Well, boys," he said then, "I've had some interesting answers to my questions about that fellow Spike Neely. He was Gulliver's cellmate in prison for a time, as you know. It seems that Spike was a bank robber."

"A bank robber!" Jupiter exclaimed.

"Exactly." Chief Reynolds nodded. "In fact, he was sent to prison for robbing a bank in San Francisco six years ago. He got away with about fifty thousand dollars in bills of large denominations. He was eventually caught, about a month later, in Chicago. An alert teller in the bank had noticed when he demanded the money that he had a slight speech defect — had trouble pronouncing the letter L. This tripped him up when a policeman in Chicago questioned him.

"However, and this seems to be the big point, the money was never recovered. He hid it and hid it well. Nobody could even get him to admit he had stolen it. Undoubtedly he planned to leave it hidden until he got out of prison and then recover it.

"Now let's take this whole thing step by step. Six years ago, Spike was captured in Chicago, about a month after the bank robbery. He probably hid the money in Chicago, but he could have hidden it right here in the Los Angeles area.

"You see, the police learned that before he went to Chicago he spent a week hiding in the home of his sister in Los Angeles. Her name is

Mrs. Miller — Mrs. Mary Miller. She was questioned at the time, but she couldn't tell the police anything helpful. She's a very respectable woman. Until the police came, she never even knew her brother was a bank robber.

"Thinking that Spike might have hidden the money in her house before he went to Chicago, the police searched it thoroughly. They didn't find anything. As he arrived there the same day he pulled the robbery up in San Francisco, he must have had the money with him. So the official theory is that Spike hid the money in Chicago."

"In the letter he wrote to Gulliver a year ago, he mentions a cousin, Danny Street, in Chicago," Jupiter put in. "Could he have left the money with him?"

"The prison authorities thought of that, Jupiter. As you suspected, they read the letter to Gulliver very carefully before they mailed it. In fact, they wired Chicago to investigate Danny Street. But the Chicago police couldn't find anyone named Street who had the slightest connection with Spike Neely.

"They finally decided the letter was harmless, so they mailed it. First, they analyzed it every which way for a secret message, but they couldn't find any."

"Neither could I," Jupiter admitted. He was pinching his lip to put his mental machinery in high gear. "Just the same, I deduce that some other criminals, learning of the letter, suspected it actually did tell where the money is, somehow. So they took to shadowing The Great Gulliver. That's when he got frightened and disappeared."

"Or was killed," Chief Reynolds said gravely. "I think it's plain that Gulliver never found the money. But someone may have tried to make him tell where it was, and got angry when he wouldn't — because he couldn't. On the other hand, he may have just taken alarm and gone into hiding, leaving his trunk behind."

"He must have suspected Spike Neely was trying to tell him something." Jupiter was thinking hard. "Otherwise why would he hide the letter? Let's suppose he just disappeared. Then these other criminals, who are still around, read in the paper of my buying Gulliver's trunk. They believed that there might be a clue to the stolen money in the trunk.

"That first night, they tried to steal it but were foiled because Uncle Titus had hidden it. Then they took to following me around. They were watching the salvage yard, figuring how to get their hands on the trunk, when they saw us sell it to Maximilian the Mystic. So they followed Mr. Maximilian, forced his car off the road, and stole the trunk."

"They sure wanted that trunk badly!" Pete exclaimed. "I'm glad we got rid of it in time."

"You really should have brought the trunk to me," the Chief pointed out.

"We suggested that, sir, to Mr. Maximilian," Jupiter answered. "He wouldn't hear of it. He wanted the trunk. And of course we didn't know anyone would actually injure him to get it. Besides, we couldn't find any clue in it."

"Well, what's done is done," Chief Reynolds said. "But all this talk has been leading up to a very important point. We're agreed, aren't we, that these criminals think there's a clue to the missing money in that trunk?"

The boys all nodded.

"Well," the Chief continued, "now the crooks have the trunk. They've searched it carefully. They haven't found any clue. So what do you suppose they think now?"

Jupiter caught on first and swallowed hard. Seeing that Pete didn't get what the Chief meant, Bob burst out, "They think we found the clue and took it out of the trunk before we sold it to Mr. Maximilian! They think that we — that we still have the clue to all that money!"

"But gleeps!" Pete objected. "We don't! We don't know a thing!"

"I know that," the Chief said. "And you know that. But if these fellows *think* you have the clue — well, they might still come around and try to force you to give it to them."

They thought about this. It wasn't a pleasant idea.

"You mean we could still be in danger, Chief?" Jupiter said at last.

"I'm afraid so." Chief Reynolds spoke seriously. "So I want you to keep alert. If you see anyone who looks suspicious hanging around the salvage yard, call me at once. Or if anyone gets in touch with you about the trunk, let me know. Will you do that?"

"We certainly will!" Bob promised.

"There's one problem," Jupe said, frowning. "A lot of strangers come to the salvage yard as customers. It's hard to tell if any of them are suspicious. But if we notice anyone who does seem suspicious, we'll notify you immediately."

"Be sure you do," Chief Reynolds said.

In a very thoughtful mood, The Three Investigators left police headquarters and rode back to the salvage yard.

JUPE TACKLES
THE CASE

"More and more I like this whole business less and less!" Pete exploded. "I don't want any tough characters thinking we have a clue we don't have. There's no telling what they might do. People like that don't listen to reason."

"And we thought we were getting rid of all our troubles by getting rid of the trunk," Bob added. "Got any ideas, Jupe?"

The Three Investigators were secluded in the workshop of the salvage yard and none of them looked happy. Even Jupiter's round face was creased by a frown.

"I'm afraid," he said, "that these men, who-ever they are, won't quit until the money is found. The best way to solve our problem would be to find the money ourselves and turn it over to the police, with plenty of newspaper publicity. Then they'd give up."

"Great! Just great!" Pete retorted sarcastically. "All we have to do is find some money that's been hidden for years. Money that the police and the Treasury Department agents haven't been able to find. Nothing to it. Easy as falling off a log. Let's do it before dinner so we can wrap this whole case up."

"Pete's right," Bob said. "I mean, what chance have we of finding any hidden money when we don't even have a clue to it?"

"It certainly won't be easy," Jupiter admitted. "But I think we have to try. We won't have any peace of mind until the money is found. We're investigators — it'll be a real challenge to us."

Pete groaned.

"How would we start, Jupe?" Bob asked.

"First we have to assume that the money is hidden someplace here in the Los Angeles region," Jupiter said slowly. "Obviously, if it's hidden in Chicago we haven't a chance of finding it."

Pete's expression said he didn't think they had a chance anyway.

"Next," Jupiter said, "we have to find out all we can about Spike Neely's actions when he was hiding out at his sister's house. That means we must locate the sister, Mrs. Miller, and ask her to tell us everything she can."

"But Chief Reynolds said the police questioned her at the time," Bob protested. "If they didn't learn anything, how can we?"

"I don't know," Jupiter told him. "But we have to try. It's our only lead. I know it's a long shot, but when there's nothing else to do, you have to try the long shot. Just possibly we might think of some questions the police forgot to ask."

"I wish you'd never read that piece in the paper about the auction," Pete muttered. "All right, how do we start?"

"First," Jupiter began, but he was interrupted by his aunt's powerful voice calling to them.

"Boys! Lunch! Come and get it while it's hot."

Pete jumped up. "That's the first thing I've heard today that I've liked!" he exclaimed. "Let's eat. Then we can think about your idea, Jupe."

In a few minutes the boys were seated in Aunt Mathilda's kitchen. Mrs. Jones bustled about serving them generous helpings of franks and beans. Presently Titus Jones came in and joined them.

"Well, Jupiter, my boy," he said, "what have you been up to now? Making friends with Gypsies, have you?"

"Gypsies?" Jupiter looked up, startled, and Bob and Pete paused with forks half raised.

"There were a couple of Gypsies in the yard this morning," Titus Jones explained. "While you lads were downtown. Oh, they didn't say they were Gypsies, and they weren't dressed like Gypsies, but I could tell. After all, when I was with the circus I saw a lot of them."

During his younger years, Mr. Jones had traveled with a small circus, taking tickets and playing the steam calliope that every circus had in those days.

"They were looking for me?" Jupiter asked.

"I guess it was you." His uncle chuckled. "They said they had a message from a friend for the fat one. I know you're not fat, Jupiter, just stocky and well-muscled, but for some reason people do call you fat."

"What was the message?" Jupiter asked, ignoring his uncle's chuckles.

"It was more like a riddle," Mr. Jones replied. "Let me see now, what they said was, 'A frog in a pond with hungry fish must jump hard to get out.' Does it mean anything to you?"

Jupiter gulped slightly. Bob and Pete swallowed hard.

"I'm not sure," Jupiter answered. "Maybe it's an old Gypsy proverb. You're sure they were Gypsies?"

"Positive," his uncle said. "I've seen enough to know. Besides, as they left I heard them talking in Romany — that's the old Gypsy language. I couldn't understand everything they said, but I heard what sounded like 'danger,' then 'keep a sharp eye.' I certainly hope you aren't involved in anything dangerous."

"Gypsies!" Mrs. Jones snorted, seating herself at the table. "Jupiter, now that you've gotten rid of that horrible old skull, don't tell me you're getting mixed up with Gypsies somehow."

"No, Aunt Mathilda," Jupiter answered. "At least I don't think I am."

"Well, they seemed friendly." Titus Jones stated, helping himself to more franks.

The three boys finished eating in silence, and then returned to Headquarters.

"A Gypsy message," Pete said hollowly. "'A frog in a pond with hungry fish must jump hard to get out.' Does that mean what I think it means?"

Jupiter nodded. "I'm afraid so. It's a veiled

warning to us that we'd better work hard to solve this case. I wish I knew where the Gypsies fitted into this, though. First I talked to Zelda. Then Zelda and all her people disappeared. Now two Gypsies show up to leave a message for me, from a friend. I surmise that Zelda is the friend, but I wish she wouldn't be so mysterious."

"Me too," Pete said, and sighed.

"Well, what do we do now?" Bob asked.

"We talk to Spike Neely's sister," Jupiter said. "We know she lives in Los Angeles. Maybe she's in the phone book."

Pete handed him the telephone book and Jupe found there were several Mary Millers listed. Starting with the first one, Jupiter began phoning. In a deep voice that sounded quite adult, he said he wished to contact Mr. Spike Neely. The first three women he called said they'd never heard of Spike Neely, but the fourth replied that Spike Neely was dead and it was impossible to contact him. Jupiter said "Thank you" and hung up.

"We've located the right Mrs. Miller," he told the others. "Her address is over in Hollywood, in one of the older sections. I propose we visit her immediately and see if she can give us any information."

"It seems like an awfully long shot to me," Pete muttered. "What can she tell us that she didn't tell the police at the time?"

"I don't know," Jupiter said, "but 'a frog in a pool with hungry fish must jump hard to get out.'"

"I guess you're right," Bob said. "How will we get there? It's too far to ride on our bikes."

"We'll call the Rent-'n-Ride Auto Agency and ask for the use of Worthington and the Rolls-Royce," Jupiter said.

Some time earlier, Jupiter had entered a contest and won the use of a magnificent old Rolls for a short time. Later, the generosity of a boy whom they had helped allowed them to continue to use the car occasionally. However, when Jupiter phoned now, he learned that the car and Worthington, the chauffeur, were both out of town with a customer.

"Well, if we can't use the Rolls-Royce," he said to the others, "we'll ask Uncle Titus to lend us Konrad and the light truck. Things aren't busy today so he probably won't mind."

But it turned out that Mr. Jones first had an errand for Konrad and the truck. Konrad would not be free for several hours, so the boys decided to put in the time repainting some furniture. They worked in a spot where they could watch

91

everyone who came into the yard, keeping alert for anyone who looked suspicious. But no one seemed in the least interested in them.

Finally Konrad came back with the truck and unloaded it. All three boys squeezed into the front seat beside him, Bob sitting on Pete's lap, and they set off for Hollywood.

Mrs. Miller's home turned out to be an attractive bungalow with a palm tree and two banana trees outside it. Jupiter pushed the doorbell and a pleasant-looking middle-aged woman came to the door.

"Yes?" she said. "If you're selling subscriptions, I'm sorry but I don't need any more magazines."

"It's not that, ma'am," Jupiter said. "May I give you one of our cards?" And he handed her one of The Three Investigators' official business cards.

Mrs. Miller looked at it, puzzled.

"You boys are investigators?" she asked. "It hardly seems possible."

"You might call us junior investigators," Jupiter said. "Here's another card that the police gave us."

He let Mrs. Miller see the card Chief Reynolds had given him at the time of an earlier adventure. This one said:

This certifies that the bearer is a Volunteer Junior Assistant Deputy cooperating with the police force of Rocky Beach. Any assistance given him will be appreciated.

(Signed) Samuel Reynolds
Chief of Police

"My, that certainly does look impressive," Mrs. Miller said. "But why are you calling on me?"

"We hope you can help us," Jupiter said frankly. "We're in a little trouble and we need some information. It has to do with your brother, Spike Neely. It's quite a long story, but if you'd let us come in I could explain better."

Mrs. Miller hesitated, then held the door open.

"All right," she said. "You look like respectable boys. I hoped I'd heard the last of Spike, but I'll try to help you."

A few moments later they were seated on the sofa in her living room. Jupiter was explaining as well as he could the curious set of events that had begun with his buying an old trunk at auction. He left out any reference to Socrates, however, as a talking skull would be hard for anyone else to take.

"So you see," he finished, "someone apparently thinks there was a clue in Gulliver's trunk to where the money is hidden. Because we had the trunk for a time, they may think we found the clue and know where the money is. They might — well, they might try to make us tell them, and we can't. You can see what a problem it is."

"Goodness, yes," the woman said. "But I don't see how I can help you. I never knew anything about the money, as I told the police at the time. Why, I never dreamed that my brother was a criminal until the police came looking for him."

"If you could tell us what you told the police at the time," Jupiter suggested, "we might spot some clue."

"Well, I'll try. It was six years ago, you know, but I can remember quite clearly. Frank — that was Spike's real name — and I hadn't seen much of each other since he left home when he was eighteen. Once in a long while he'd come to see me and my husband for a few days, but he never said anything about what he was doing.

"I realize now that he was probably hiding out after committing a robbery, but at the time I just thought he was restless and liked to travel. When I asked him what his work was, he said he

94

was a salesman. But, whenever he was staying with us, he used to help my husband out.

"My husband had a one-man home-repair business. He was a very good workman. If you needed your house painted, he could paint it. If it needed wallpapering, he'd do that too. Or lay a new floor. Or install a bathroom. He could do anything around the house and he made good money.

"As I said, when Spike visited us, he helped on whatever job my husband might have at the time. But this time he didn't seem to want to go out of the house. He seemed nervous. His speech defect was worse than usual. You know that's how he was finally caught — he had trouble pronouncing the letter L in words. For instance, if he said 'flower,' it came out 'f'ower.'

"Anyway, I know now that he was hiding out after the bank robbery in San Francisco. So for almost a week Spike stayed home by himself — I had a job then too.

"He did make himself useful. He painted and papered the downstairs. You know how it is — a busy workman like my husband neglects his own home to do the outside jobs.

"But then my husband got sick. He was working on a big redecorating job for some restaurant and got too sick to finish. He asked Spike to take over for him, and Spike could hardly refuse. But I remember he dressed in baggy overalls and wore dark glasses every time he left the house.

"It took Spike several days to finish the job, and all that time my husband got worse. We were just going to move him to a hospital when he unexpectedly died."

Mrs. Miller sniffed and dabbed at her eyes a moment.

"I certainly thought Frank would stay with me then, to help me, but he didn't. He left even before the funeral. He said he had to leave in a hurry and he just packed up and went. I was very surprised. Later, I figured it out."

"You did?" Jupiter asked. "What was his reason?"

"It was the death notice in the newspaper for my husband. You know death notices always mention the next of kin, and in my husband's notice I said that he was survived by me, his wife, and a brother-in-law, Frank Neely, living at the same address. I think Frank was afraid someone would see it and know where to find him, so he hurried off.

"The next I heard of him was when the police came to question me after he was captured in Chicago. But I couldn't tell them anything. As I say, I never knew that Frank was a bank robber."

"When your brother left, did he say anything about coming back or seeing you again?" Jupiter asked.

"I don't remember anything...Yes, I do too. It's just come back to me, now that you mention it. He said, 'Sis, you're not going to sell this house or anything, are you? You'll be staying right here so I'll always know where to find you?'"

"And what did you answer, Mrs. Miller?"

"I said no, I wasn't going to sell the house. I'd be right where I was any time he came to town."

"Then I think I know where he hid the money!" Jupiter announced triumphantly. "You say he was alone here a lot while both you and your husband were out working. Then there's one logical place for him to have hidden the money — right here in this house!"

AN UNPLEASANT
SURPRISE

Both Bob and Pete looked at Jupe in amazement.

"But Chief Reynolds said the police searched the house and didn't find anything," Bob reminded him.

"Because somehow Spike Neely was too clever," Jupiter said. "He hid the money so well that an ordinary search couldn't find it. Fifty thousand dollars in large bills wouldn't make a very big package. He could have tucked it away in the attic, under the eaves, or somewhere like that. He planned to come visiting you again, Mrs. Miller, when the coast was clear, and get the money back. Only he got sent to jail and died there."

"He did ask Mrs. Miller if she was going to stay here!" Bob said excitedly. "That shows he planned to come back."

"And he had several days in which to think of a hiding place no one would suspect," Pete put in, showing some excitement himself. "It would have to be tricky, to fool the police, but I'll bet you can find it, Jupe!"

"Would you be willing to let us just look around a little, Mrs. Miller?" Jupiter asked hopefully. "Just to see if we can spot any likely place?"

Mrs. Miller shook her head.

"It does seem possible, the way you reason it out," she said, "but you couldn't ever find the money in this house." She shook her head again. "You see, this isn't the house I was living in at the time. I moved four years ago. I didn't think I ever would, but someone made me such a good offer I couldn't say no. So I sold and moved here."

Jupiter rallied from his first disappointment.

"Then it could still be in the other house," he said.

"Yes, that could be," Mrs. Miller agreed. "After all, Frank was very clever. Even though the police searched thoroughly, he might have fooled them. I used to live at 532 Danville Street. That's where you'd have to look now."

"Thank you," Jupiter said and got to his feet. "You've been a big help, Mrs. Miller. We must follow up this new information immediately."

They said their good-byes and left hastily. A moment later they were crowding again into the truck, where Konrad waited for them.

"We want to go to 532 Danville Street, Konrad," Jupiter said. "Do you know where that is?"

The big blond man dug out a worn map of Los Angeles and the towns around it. After some study they found Danville Street. It was a fairly short street but some distance away. Konrad looked doubtful.

"I think we better go home, Jupe," he said. "Mr. Titus told me not to be away too long."

"We'll just drive by the address," Jupiter said. "We'll make sure where it is. After all, I don't suppose we could just barge in and search somebody's house. We'll have to tell Chief Reynolds of our deduction."

Pete and Bob knew that Jupiter would have liked to find the money himself and take it in triumph to the authorities. But they all realized that was impossible. Konrad agreed, however, that they could drive by the address on Danville Street on their way back to Rocky Beach, and they started off.

All three boys were in much better spirits now, though Pete still had some doubts.

"After all, Jupe," he said, "we can't be positive that Spike Neely hid the money he stole in his sister's house."

Jupiter shook his head.

"It's the only logical place, Pete," he said. "It's where I would have hidden the money if I'd been Spike Neely."

After making a number of turns, they came out on Danville Street.

"This is the nine-hundred block," Jupiter announced. "Turn left, Konrad, the five-hundred block should be in that direction."

Konrad turned and all three boys watched the passing houses sharply, reading the street numbers.

"We're in the eight-hundred block now," Bob announced. "Three more blocks and we should be there."

They traveled along past a number of small, neat houses sitting on well-tended grounds. Now all three boys were leaning forward and craning their necks.

"It ought to be right in the next block," Bob said eagerly. "About the middle of the block, I'd say. On the right-hand side, of course, because that's where the even-numbered houses are."

"Stop in the middle of the next block, Konrad," Jupe directed.

"OK, Jupe," the driver agreed.

He drove a minute and stopped.

"This the place, Jupe?"

Jupiter did not answer. He was staring open-mouthed at a large apartment house that took up most of the block on the right-hand side of the street. There were no small private residences at all on that side.

"Number 532 is gone!" Bob said hollowly. "There's just that apartment house, and it's number 510."

"It looks as if we lost a house," Pete said, with a feeble attempt at humor.

"Try the next block, Konrad," Jupiter said. "Maybe number 532 is there."

But in the next block the houses were numbered in the four hundreds. There was no 532 Danville Street. Konrad pulled the truck to a stop and looked questioningly at the boys.

"Do you suppose Mrs. Miller wasn't telling us the truth?" Bob asked. "That she never lived at 532 Danville Street at all? Maybe back where we left her she's tearing the house apart looking for that fifty thousand dollars. Maybe she was just trying to get rid of us."

"No," Jupiter said. "I believe Mrs. Miller was telling us the truth. Something has happened to number 532. You two wait here. I shall make a quick investigation to see if I can find out what."

Jupiter slid out of the truck and disappeared. After some minutes he returned, puffing slightly.

"Well," he said, "I learned something anyway. I talked to the superintendent of the apartment house. He's been there ever since it was built. He says it was built nearly four years ago, and that six houses in the block were moved to make room for it."

"Moved!" Pete exclaimed. "Moved where?"

"To Maple Street. That's about three blocks away, parallel with this street. The houses were in good condition and not too big so instead of being torn down they were moved over to vacant lots along Maple Street and put on new foundations. Mrs. Miller's house is still around — it's just in a new location."

"Good grief!" Bob said. "A traveling house! How can we find it? It won't be numbered 532 anymore. It'll have a new street number."

"Well," Jupiter said, "we can telephone Mrs. Miller and ask her to describe it to us. Then we can go over to Maple Street and look for it."

"We can't do that today," Bob pointed out. "It's getting too late."

"Yup, Jupe, got to get back to the yard,"

Konrad put in. "We are late now."

"Well, we'll do it tomorrow," Jupiter said. "All right, Konrad, let's go home."

Konrad started the motor and pulled away from the curb. As he did so, a large black car with three very hard-faced men in it also pulled out from the curb, a block back of them, and followed. They did not notice it, which was just as well for their peace of mind.

It was almost closing time at The Jones Salvage Yard when they got back, and Titus Jones mildly scolded them for being gone so long. Then he turned to Jupiter.

"Jupiter, my boy," he said, "while you were gone, a package came for you. Were you expecting something?"

"A package?" Jupiter looked surprised. "No, I wasn't expecting anything. What is it, Uncle Titus?"

"I don't know, my boy. It's all wrapped up, a large box, and as it is addressed to you, naturally I didn't open it. There it is, beside the office door."

All three boys rushed to the box. It was an oversize cardboard carton, securely sealed with many strips of heavy brown adhesive paper. The label on it indicated that it had come by express from Los Angeles but did not give the name of the sender.

"Golly, what do you suppose it is?" Pete asked.

"We'll have to open it to find out," Jupiter said, puzzled. "Let's take it back to the workshop and open it there."

With some difficulty he and Pete carried the box around the piles of secondhand material to the seclusion of the workshop. Jupiter produced his prized Swiss knife with many blades, swiftly cut through the strips of sealing paper, and folded back the top of the carton. Then all three stared with dismay at what was inside.

"Oh, no!" Pete groaned. "Not that!"

It took even Jupiter a moment to find his voice.

"Someone," he said, "has sent us back Gulliver's trunk."

They stared at the top of the trunk that they'd thought they were rid of forever. And as they did so, a very muffled voice spoke.

"Hurry!" it said. "Find — the clue."

Socrates! Speaking to them from inside the trunk!

THE THREE FIND
SOME CLUES

"Well, now what?" Pete asked gloomily.

It was quite late the following afternoon, a Saturday. The Three Investigators were gathered at the rear of The Jones Salvage Yard for a consultation. The previous evening they had felt no desire to investigate the riddle of the return of Gulliver's trunk. Its mysterious reappearance had, indeed, rather shaken them up. They had hidden the box behind the printing press and agreed to put off their next move until today.

Bob had just arrived from his job in the local library. Jupiter, in charge of the salvage yard while his aunt and uncle were in Los Angeles for the day, was taking advantage of a lull in business to join him and Pete.

Now they were all looking at the trunk and wondering what to do with it.

"I know what," Bob said. "Let's take the trunk right down to Chief Reynolds, tell him everything we know, and let him carry on from there."

"Good idea!" Pete agreed emphatically. "Well, Jupe, what do you say?"

"I suppose so," Jupiter said slowly. "Except that we really don't know too much. We *think* Spike Neely hid the stolen money in his sister's house, but we can't be positive. It's just a good deduction."

"It's good enough for me," Bob said. "Spike showed up at his sister's house the same day he stole the money up in San Francisco. So he must have had it with him. He was afraid of being caught, so he probably hid it before he left. He thought she'd keep right on living there, so someday when the coast was clear he could come back for it."

"Besides," Pete put in, "if he didn't hide it there, we don't know where he hid it and couldn't find it anyway. It's all we have to go on."

"Yesterday," Jupiter said, "Socrates spoke to us."

"I'll say he did!" Pete shuddered. "And believe me, I didn't like it."

"It was sort of unnerving," Bob agreed.

"But he did speak to us. At the moment I'm not even trying to figure out how," Jupiter said. "He told us to hurry and find the clue. So there must be a clue in the trunk even if we haven't spotted it yet."

"If there's a clue in it, Chief Reynolds can have the police laboratory go over it inch by inch," Pete argued. "Anyway, he may not need it. If he can locate Mrs. Miller's house on Maple Street, he can get permission to search it and probably find the money anyway."

"That's true," Jupiter agreed. "Well, all right. But first we ought to phone Mrs. Miller to ask her to describe the house, so we can tell the Chief what it looks like."

"Then let's do it!" Pete said. "On to Headquarters."

"Just a moment," said Jupe. He went out to the front of the salvage yard, saw that Hans and Konrad could handle the few customers, then followed Bob and Pete into Tunnel Two.

A minute later they were inside Headquarters. Jupiter looked up Mrs. Miller's number in the telephone book and very shortly was speaking to her.

"What did my house look like?" Mrs. Miller repeated in some surprise. "Why, my goodness, all you have to do is go to 532 Danville Street and there it is."

When told that the house had been moved, and that a large apartment house now stood on the spot, she gave a little gasp.

"An apartment house!" she said. "No wonder the man was so anxious to buy it. If I'd known the truth, maybe I'd have asked for more money. Well, anyway, it's a cute little bungalow with brown shingle siding. Just one story, but it has a little attic with a round window in front. I can't tell you anything special about it. It was just a nice, well-built little bungalow."

"Thank you," Jupiter said. "I'm sure the authorities will be able to locate it."

He hung up and looked at his two companions.

"The more I think about it," he said, "the more I feel sure that the money is hidden in Mrs. Miller's old house, but in some very tricky manner. And I'm sure there's a clue in the trunk too."

"Even if there is, I'm tired of that trunk!" Pete said firmly. "See what happened to Maximilian the Mystic. Now the trunk's come back to us, and I don't want it. It's dangerous. Let Chief Reynolds look for the clue."

"Well, we did agree to cooperate with Chief

Reynolds," Jupiter said. "So I guess the thing to do is take the trunk to him. We'd better phone to let him know we're coming."

He used the telephone again, and in a moment was connected with police headquarters.

"Chief Reynolds' office, Lieutenant Carter speaking," a crisp, unfamiliar voice answered.

"This is Jupiter Jones. May I speak to the Chief, please?"

"Chief Reynolds is away until tomorrow," Lieutenant Carter replied curtly. "Try him then."

"But this may be important," Jupiter said. "You see, I think we have a clue that — "

"Forget it, kid!" Lieutenant Carter said impatiently. "I'm very busy, and one thing I don't want is boy wonders in my hair. Maybe the Chief lets you mess around in things sometimes, but personally I think kids like you should be seen and not heard."

"But the Chief asked me — " Jupiter began.

"Take it up with him tomorrow! I have to go now!" And the phone at the other end was hung up with a bang.

Jupiter hung up also and looked blankly at Pete and Bob.

"Something tells me," Pete said, "that Lieutenant Carter doesn't like us."

"He sounded as if he didn't like anybody," Bob put in. "Especially kids."

"His attitude is quite common among adults," Jupiter said with a sigh. "They think that just because we're young we don't have any good ideas. Actually, we often have a fresh viewpoint on a problem. But I guess we can't take the trunk down to Chief Reynolds before tomorrow — maybe not even then, because tomorrow's Sunday. We may have to wait until Monday. So I suggest we search the trunk again and try to find that clue Socrates mentioned."

"I'm tired of that trunk," Pete said firmly. "I'm tired of Socrates. I don't want him talking to me."

"I don't think he'll talk to us anymore," Jupiter replied. "Somehow he doesn't seem to talk face to face. He talked to me in the dark in my room, and from inside the trunk, but never directly."

"He said 'boo' to your aunt," Bob pointed out.

"Yes. I can't explain that," Jupiter admitted. "But suppose we open the trunk and have a look. Perhaps someone took something out before returning it."

They crawled out Tunnel Two and opened the trunk. The interior looked just as it had before.

Socrates, well wrapped in old velvet, was snugly in a corner. The letter was still in place inside the tear in the lining.

Jupiter took Socrates out, unwrapped him, and set him on his ivory base on the printing press. Then he picked up the letter.

"Let's have another look at this," he said.

All three read the letter again. It seemed as innocent as before.

State Prison Hospital
July 17

Dear Gulliver:

Just a few words from your old pal and cell-mate, Spike Neely. I'm in the hospital, and it looks like I haven't got much longer.

I may last five days, or three weeks, or even two months, the doctors aren't sure. But in any case, it's time to say good-bye.

If you're ever in Chicago, look up my cousin Danny Street. Tell him hello for me. Wish I could say more, but this is all I can manage.

Your friend,
Spike

"If there's a hidden clue there, I can't find it,"

Jupiter muttered. "I wonder if — wait! I've found something. Look!"

He held out the letter and the envelope to Bob. "Do you see what we missed?"

"What we missed?" Bob looked puzzled. "No, I don't see anything special, Jupe."

"The stamps on the envelope!" Jupe said. *"We didn't look under the stamps for a message!"*

Bob looked at the two stamps — a two-cent stamp and a four-cent stamp. He took the envelope and ran his finger over them. His expression changed to one of great excitement.

"Jupe!" he exclaimed. "You're right! There's something under one of these stamps. The four-cent stamp feels just a little bit thicker than the two."

Pete also ran his finger over the stamps and nodded. The four-cent stamp was just a trifle thicker — not enough for the eye to notice unless you looked very closely.

"Let's get inside Headquarters and steam these stamps off and see what's underneath!" Bob exclaimed.

They scrambled back through Tunnel Two and within three minutes had a little kettle boiling in the laboratory. Jupiter held the corner of the envelope in the steam until the stamps loosened. Then he gave a shout of excitement.

"Look!" he cried. "There's another stamp underneath the four. A green one-cent stamp."

"That's queer." Bob frowned. "What does it mean, Jupe?"

"I can tell you what it means," Pete said. "There's nothing mysterious about it. Don't you remember that back about the time this letter was mailed, the postage rates went up by a cent? Spike Neely probably put a one-cent stamp on, then realized that wouldn't be enough so he pasted on a two, then put the four-cent stamp on top of the one."

"Gosh, that could be right," Bob said. "I think Pete has hit on it, Jupe."

"I'm not so sure." Jupe scowled at the green stamp on the envelope. Then, carefully, he peeled it off. "There may be writing underneath it," he said.

"No," Bob announced when the stamp was off. "No writing. None on the back of any of the stamps either. What do you say now, Jupe?"

"It's too peculiar to be an accident," Jupe said, still scowling. "It has to mean something."

"Then what?" Pete demanded.

"I'm thinking," Jupiter said. "Spike knew this letter would be censored. So I deduce he used the stamps to send his message. He put one stamp under another stamp, so neatly it wouldn't be noticed. He expected Gulliver to examine the whole letter very carefully and find it. I deduce that the one-cent stamp, being green, the color of U.S. paper money, stands for the missing fifty thousand dollars. What Spike meant — "

He broke off, thinking hard. Bob's shout broke the silence.

"I've got it!" he yelled. "A stamp is a piece of paper, see? Money is paper too. Spike put a piece of paper underneath another piece of paper. Spike was telling Gulliver that the money was hidden someplace under some paper.

"Mrs. Miller told us that while Spike was hiding out in her old house, he papered the whole downstairs! That was when he hid the fifty thousand dollars. He put the bills side by side and pasted them underneath the new wallpaper!"

"Wow!" Pete said admiringly. "Bob, you've got it. That has to be the answer, doesn't it, Jupe?"

Jupiter nodded. "Yes," he said. "Remarkable deduction, Bob. I'm just remembering a story I once read. It's a mystery story by a man named Robert Barr. In it a character named Lord Chizelrigg hides a lot of gold by beating it into gold-leaf and pasting it under some wallpaper. The principle is the same. Only Spike Neely used paper money, which is much easier to handle."

"But wait a minute!" Bob put in. "Mrs. Miller said Spike Neely went out and finished a job for Mr. Miller. Maybe he hid the money there."

"I don't think so." Jupiter shook his head. "The best place would be — Oh! Oh! Oh!"

"Oh! Oh! Oh! what?" Pete asked. "What're you oh-ing about, Jupe?"

"Spike tells us! That is, he told Gulliver. Right in the letter. Look at it!" Jupiter handed the letter over to Bob and Pete.

"See what he starts off by saying. *'I may last five days, or three weeks, or even two months.'* Take those numbers and put them together. They make 532. What does that remind you of?"

"That was the number of Mrs. Miller's house!" Bob shouted. "532 Danville Street."

"Right," Jupiter said. "And look here. He tells Gulliver, *'If you're ever in Chicago, look up my cousin Danny Street.'*"

"Danny could be a nickname for Danville!" Pete exclaimed.

"Right!" Jupe agreed. "That mention of a cousin, and Chicago, is just put in to distract attention from the words *Danny Street*. As near as he dared say it, Spike Neely was telling Gulliver that the money was hidden at 532 Danville Street."

"Under the wallpaper!" Bob chimed in. "He didn't dare say too much, but that was very tricky, putting one stamp under another!"

"We've solved the riddle," Pete said, jubilant. Then he looked thoughtful. "Now how do we find the money?"

"If it's underneath somebody's wallpaper, we can't just barge in and say, 'Excuse us, we have to rip your wallpaper off,' " Bob remarked.

"No," Jupiter agreed. "That's a job for the police. We'll have to tell Chief Reynolds. It's no use trying to tell Lieutenant Carter — he doesn't want us bothering him. Tomorrow, though, or Monday, when the Chief is back — "

The ringing of the telephone interrupted him. Startled, Jupiter picked it up.

"Three Investigators, Jupiter Jones speaking," he said.

"Good!" answered a man's authoritative voice. "This is George Grant speaking."

"George Grant?" Jupiter frowned. The name was unfamiliar to him.

"That's right. Chief Reynolds told you I'd be getting in touch with you, didn't he?"

"Why, no," Jupiter said, puzzled. "He didn't mention you, Mr. Grant."

"He must have forgotten," the man said. "It was he who gave me your telephone number. I'm a special agent for the Bankers' Protective Association. I've been keeping an eye on you since I read in the paper about your buying that trunk of The Great Gulliver's. And —"

"Yes?" Jupiter asked, a bit uneasily, as the man paused.

"Do you boys know that three of the worst thugs in California are watching you day and night?"

DISTURBING
NEWS

"W-watching us?" Jupiter's voice quavered slightly. Pete and Bob gulped.

"They certainly are. Watching you and following you. Their names are Three-Finger Munger, Baby-Face Benson, and Leo the Knife. They were in prison with Spike Neely, and they're hoping that you'll lead them to the money he hid before he was caught."

"We — we haven't seen anyone watching us, Mr. Grant."

"Of course not. These men are professionals. They've rented a house down the road from the salvage yard and are watching it through field glasses. If you go anyplace, they follow you."

"We'd better tell the police," Jupiter said, alarmed. Bob and Pete, listening to the little loudspeaker, nodded hard.

"I've already told Chief Reynolds," Mr. Grant said. "He offered to chase them away, but said he couldn't arrest them because watching you isn't illegal. They haven't actually done anything — yet."

"Chief Reynolds was afraid some criminals might think we knew where the missing money is," Jupiter said, none too happily. "I guess that's why they're watching us. To see if we go get it."

"I hope you don't try," Mr. Grant said. "No telling what Three-Finger and the others might attempt. If you actually have any clue, take my advice and turn it over to the police."

"But we haven't," Jupiter said. "That is, we didn't have."

"But you do now?" Mr. Grant asked.

"Well — yes," Jupiter admitted. "We just found a clue that seems significant."

"Good work!" the man said heartily. "Take it right down to Chief Reynolds. I'll meet you there and we'll all have a confab.... Uh-oh, that won't work. I just remembered that the Chief is out of town today."

"That's right," Jupiter agreed. "We tried to

telephone him. Lieutenant Carter is taking his place. The Lieutenant wouldn't even listen to us."

"And if you did go to him now, he'd probably take all the credit and keep you from getting the reward," Mr. Grant said thoughtfully.

"Reward?" Jupiter asked. Bob and Pete looked excitedly at each other.

"The Bankers' Protective Association has offered a ten percent reward to anyone who can locate the missing money. That's five thousand dollars that you'd be entitled to. That is, if your clue is a good one."

"Five thousand dollars!" Pete whispered to Jupe. "That idea I like! Ask him how we can win it."

"I have an idea," Grant continued. "If you lay your information before the Bankers' Protective Association directly and we pass it on to the police, you're in line for the reward. It's on record that you supplied the clue. I could come see you and — No, that's not a good idea.

"If those thugs saw me, they'd probably recognize me, and they might make some desperate move. Suppose you come see me secretly. I'm in town now."

"I can't leave the salvage yard," Jupiter answered, scowling. "I'm supposed to be in charge here. My aunt and uncle won't be back for an hour or two."

"Hmmm — I see." Mr. Grant was silent for a moment. "Do you think you can slip away later this evening, after you close? All three of you meet me somewhere? You'd have to get away without Three-Finger and the others seeing you go."

"I believe I could do that, sir," Jupiter agreed. "Of course, Bob and Pete have to leave soon to go home for dinner. Do you think they'll be followed?"

"I doubt it. You're the one the crooks are interested in. You're sure you can slip away without being seen?"

"Yes, sir. I'm sure I can," said Jupiter, thinking of Red Gate Rover, the boys' secret exit in the back fence of the yard. "It'll be late, though, because today is Saturday and the yard is open until seven o'clock."

"Excellent. Will eight o'clock be all right then?"

"Yes, Mr. Grant, I think so."

"Then suppose we meet in the park — Oceanview Park. I'll be sitting on a bench inside the east entrance, reading a newspaper. I'll have on a brown sports jacket and a brown snap-brim hat. You three get there separately, making sure you're not being followed. That clear?"

"Yes, sir," Jupiter said.

"And don't breathe a word to anyone before we meet. It's important that nothing leaks out until I have your statement. Bring your clues with you. Check?"

"All clear, Mr. Grant," Jupiter agreed.

"Then I'll see you at eight. Good-bye until then."

As Jupiter hung up, Pete let out a suppressed exclamation.

"Wow! A five-thousand-dollar reward. What's the matter, Jupe, why don't you look happy?"

"We haven't found the money yet," Jupiter said.

"We're bound to find it. Or anyway the police are after Mr. Grant gives them our information. Maybe they'll let us come along when they hunt for it."

"Not if that Lieutenant Carter has anything to say about it," said Bob.

"I wish Chief Reynolds wasn't away today," Jupiter said. "I'd like to have him in on this. But if he knows Mr. Grant — "

A voice calling interrupted him.

"Jupe! The customers need some change!"

"That's Konrad," Jupiter said. "I'd better get

back on the job. I'm supposed to be in charge. Bob and Pete, can you repack the trunk and put Socrates away?"

"Golly!" Bob looked at his watch. "I've got to get to the library before it closes, Jupe. I left my jacket there when I quit work. Then I'd better get on home."

"It's okay. I'll pack the trunk," Pete said. "Then I'd better get home too. We'll all meet at the park at eight o'clock. Right?"

"Right," Jupiter said.

They all left Headquarters and separated. Pete approached the trunk and Socrates without enthusiasm.

"Well!" he challenged the skull. "What have you got to say now that we've found the clue?"

Socrates grinned at him and remained silent.

BOB SPRINGS A BOMBSHELL

Bursting with some new information, Bob pedaled furiously through the back streets of Rocky Beach, heading in a roundabout way for the meeting place in the park. He was a little late. He had taken time after dinner to look through a pile of old newspapers in the garage. He had found the special item he wanted, and now he was trying to make up for lost time. But when he got to the east entrance to the park, he saw that Pete and Jupiter were ahead of him. They were seated on a bench with a young, well-dressed man, talking earnestly. They looked up as Bob approached, his bicycle brakes squealing.

"Sorry I'm late," Bob said, puffing. "I had to hunt for something."

"You have to be Bob Andrews," the man said pleasantly. "I'm George Grant." They shook hands, and the young man extended a wallet open to show an engraved card behind a plastic window. "Here's my identification, Bob. Just to be formal."

The card said that George Grant was an accredited investigator for the Bankers' Protective Association. Bob nodded and Mr. Grant put it away.

"Jupe — " Bob started to say, but Jupiter spoke first.

"We've just been telling Mr. Grant what we learned from the letter, about the money being hidden under the wallpaper in Mrs. Miller's old house."

"You boys have done a fine job," Mr. Grant said. "The Bankers' Protective Association will be glad to see that you get the reward. If the money is pasted under the wallpaper, it's no wonder the police didn't find it when they searched the house.

"However, we have a little problem. The house is undoubtedly occupied. It'll take special police authority to enter it and rip off the wall-paper. I'm not sure —"

Bob was unable to hold back his news any longer.

"That's just it, Mr. Grant," he burst out. "If the house is still standing, it isn't occupied, and it won't be standing much longer!"

The others looked at him in amazement. He hurried on to explain.

"When I went back to the library to get my jacket, I heard a woman telling the librarian about having to get out of her house on Maple Street, and her trouble finding a new place. She finally moved down here to Rocky Beach. I asked the librarian about it and she told me there had been a piece in the paper last week. I looked it up in the copy at the library. Then I found the paper at home and cut out the story. Here it is!"

He thrust a folded piece of newspaper into Jupiter's hand. Jupiter unfolded it, and he and Mr. Grant and Pete all read it swiftly.

DEMOLITION BEGINS
FOR NEW FREEWAY

More than 300 homes, some of them new and attractive, stand

empty and silent today, awaiting the bulldozers of the wreckers. Soon they will be only memories to the residents who have had to move out of them, to make way for the freeway extension that will rise in their place.

A fifteen-block length of Maple Street will vanish, to be replaced by a six-lane freeway designed to speed the ever-increasing load of traffic through Los Angeles. Not only Maple Street will be affected, but nearby houses on the cross streets will also go.

The heartbreak to the residents who have had to move from their homes is new to them, but it is only a repetition of thousands of similar cases since the freeway program in this city began. The urgent need to keep traffic flowing through the city has meant the destruction of many thousands of homes to make way for the freeways.

There was more to the story, but Mr. Grant, having read that much, whistled softly.

"Maple Street!" he said. "That's where you

said Mrs. Miller's house was moved to four years ago, Jupiter."

"That's what the apartment-house superintendent told me," Jupiter answered.

"And now most of Maple Street is going to be demolished," Mr. Grant said. "That changes things. That means the house is empty. It means we have no time for delay. Why, Three-Finger and the others could be there now. They may have already been there and gotten the money!"

"How could that be, Mr. Grant?" Pete asked.

"They followed you boys yesterday," Mr. Grant said. "They must have followed you to Mrs. Miller's present home and deduced you were getting information from her. Then they undoubtedly followed you to the apartment house. They could easily have seen Jupiter go in to question the superintendent, and could have learned what the superintendent told him. They may have deduced that you think the money is in the house. They could be looking for it now!"

"Gosh, that's right!" Bob exclaimed. "Maybe we're too late!"

"Ordinarily I'd call on the police for help," Mr. Grant said. "But time is short and I think the only thing to do is to make a beeline for Maple Street and try to locate the house, and see if we can rescue the money immediately. No time to get in touch with the police. You boys can come with me — in fact, I need you, because you have an idea of what Mrs. Miller's former house looks like and I don't."

"That's fine, Mr. Grant," Jupiter said. "But how will we go?"

"I have a car parked around the corner. We'll go in that. You can leave your bikes here and we'll pick them up later. OK?"

Wasting no time, Pete and Bob locked their bicycles. Jupiter had walked, after slipping out of the salvage yard through Red Gate Rover. Mr. Grant led them to his car, a black station wagon, and a moment later they were off. Mr. Grant headed for Hollywood by a back route over the hills.

"You're sure the money is hidden under the wallpaper?" he asked Jupiter as they sped along.

"I'm almost positive," Jupiter said. "Mrs. Miller told us that while Spike Neely was staying with her, he did some papering and painting. He could have pasted the bills up and put wallpaper over them then.

"Then when he was in the hospital, he sneaked the address of the house into his letter. But he couldn't think of any way to tell Gulliver about the hiding place except by pasting one stamp under the other."

"Paper under paper," Mr. Grant nodded. "It figures. If we locate the money, we'll have to get some equipment to steam the wallpaper off. Luckily this is Saturday, and some of the stores are open late. But first we have to find it — and find it first!"

He kept the station wagon moving at high speed until they reached a built-up district, then he slowed.

"Now let's see that city map in the glove compartment," he told Jupiter. He came to a stop as Jupiter found the map and gave it to him. He studied the map for a moment.

"Good," he said. "We can go straight ahead until we come to Houston Avenue, then cut across on it to Maple Street. You said the five-hundred block?"

"Either that or the six-hundred block, the superintendent thought," Jupiter told him.

"We'll find it," Mr. Grant said grimly. "Lucky we still have some daylight left."

The daylight was fading fast, however, by the time they came to Houston Avenue. Mr. Grant turned left, and they proceeded for some thirty or forty blocks until they reached Maple Street.

Even though no street signs were still up, they

had no trouble telling that it was the right street. Their way was almost blocked by a mass of wreckage. The houses on one corner were already down, mere heaps of rubble waiting to be carted away. Down the blocks to their left they could see that the houses were already gone. Two huge cranes with clam buckets, which could chew up the wooden houses with their diesel-powered jaws, were parked in an open space, together with several bulldozers. A building that had once been a restaurant stood forlornly on the corner beside them as they stopped to survey the scene. Already the cranes had taken a couple of bites out of the front. It looked as if it had been bombed.

"Wow!" Pete voiced their thoughts. "It sure is a mess. Do you think we're in time, Mr. Grant?"

"Just barely," the investigator said grimly. "If I have it figured right, the five- and six-hundred blocks are a couple of streets up to our right. Let's see."

He eased the car around the rubble and turned right. In a moment they were going past houses that had not yet been torn down, but stood silent and dark with no sign of life in them.

Only a few hundred feet away was the busy

city, but here on Maple Street there was an eerie quality of desertion. The people had all gone. In a few months a concrete freeway would run through here, carrying thousands of cars. But now they had the street to themselves, except for a skinny cat that ran across the road.

"The nine-hundred block," Mr. Grant said with satisfaction. "We'll be in the six-hundred block in no time. Keep a sharp eye out for the house."

They drove slowly along, past the silent houses. Here and there a door swung open, as if to say it no longer mattered whether doors were shut or not.

"Six-hundred block," Mr. Grant announced tensely. "See anything?"

"There it is!" Pete almost shouted, pointing to a neat bungalow halfway down the block.

"There's another one that looks almost like it," Jupiter put in, pointing to the other side of the street. "Both have round windows up in the attic storage space."

"Two of them, eh?" Mr. Grant frowned. "And you don't know which is the right one?"

"Mrs. Miller just said it was a one-story bungalow with brown shingles and a round window in the attic."

"It's a common type of house here," Mr.

Grant muttered. "Let's keep going. We'll survey the next block."

In the next block they spotted another brown-shingled bungalow, standing between two stuccoed homes. This one also had a round upper window. Mr. Grant brought the car to a halt.

"Three possibilities," he said. "That makes it harder. But we seem to be here first. I don't see any cars parked on this street, nor any sign that Three-Finger and the others have beat us to it. We'll park on a side street so we won't be conspicuous, and then we'll just have to investigate all three houses until we find the right one."

THE SEARCH
BEGINS

It was almost dark as they approached the first of the brown-shingled bungalows. Mr. Grant cast a quick look up and down the block. No one was in sight on silent, deserted Maple Street.

He tried the door. It wouldn't open.

"Locked," he said. "But as it's going to be torn down, we don't have to be careful how we get in."

He took a small wrecking bar he had carried from the car and inserted the thin end between the front door and the door jamb. As he pressed, wood splintered and the door sprang open.

He entered with The Three Investigators at his heels. Inside it was quite dark. Mr. Grant flashed a light on a wall. They were in a dusty room with a few papers littering the floor. It was apparently the living room.

"We might as well start here," he said. "Though I'd expect the hiding place to be in a back room or maybe the hall. Got a knife, Jupiter?"

Jupiter brought out his prized Swiss knife and opened the big blade. He made a cut in the flowered wallpaper on the nearest wall. Mr. Grant eased the edge of a putty knife into the cut and turned back a strip of the paper. Underneath was only plaster.

"Not here," he said. "We'll have to try different spots on this wall, then the other walls, then go to the other rooms."

He and Jupiter repeated the process several feet away. Again there was nothing beneath the paper but plaster. They went around all four walls of the room, testing each in several spots. Each time they drew a blank.

"All right, now we'll try the dining room," Mr. Grant said.

The flashlight beam showing the way, they proceeded to the dining room. Jupiter made a cut and Mr. Grant turned the edge of the paper back. Pete gave a yip.

"Something green underneath!" he said.

"Jupiter, shine the light close," Mr. Grant said. "Maybe we've found it!"

Jupiter brought the light to within inches of the uncovered space. A checked green surface showed.

"Just another layer of wallpaper," Mr. Grant said. "Well, we'll look underneath it."

Underneath, however, was plaster wall again.

They finished with the dining room and went into the first bedroom. Their tests were still negative. The second bedroom was the same. The bathroom and kitchen had painted walls. Jupiter climbed a narrow ladder to the small attic. There was no wallpaper up there.

"Well, we didn't hit the jackpot on this one." Mr. Grant's voice was tense and he was sweating a little. "Let's try the next house."

They emerged into darkness. Only the street lights at each corner still were on. The houses were all dark and very spooky. Mr. Grant led the boys to the next block and the first brown-shingled bungalow there. The front door was unlocked this time.

Inside, the layout was much the same as in the first house. But the wallpaper looked newer.

"Maybe this is it," Mr. Grant said hopefully. "Make a cut, Jupiter."

Jupiter again cut into the wallpaper, Mr. Grant turned it back — and there was nothing underneath.

In growing excitement, they moved through the rest of the house, swiftly testing all the walls in different places. They found nothing.

"That leaves just one more house," said Mr. Grant. His voice was slightly hoarse. "That has to be it!"

He led the way across the street to the third bungalow that fitted Mrs. Miller's description. As Mr. Grant prepared to force the locked door, Jupiter flashed a light onto the door frame. Metal street numbers screwed into the white woodwork around the door reflected the light.

"Don't do that!" Mr. Grant said sharply. "We don't want to attract any attention."

"But I think I've spotted something," Jupiter said. "I think this used to be Mrs. Miller's house."

"How can you tell, Jupe?" Bob said, almost whispering. The dark desertion of the street somehow made whispering seem proper.

"Yes, how can you tell?" Mr. Grant asked.

"This house is number 671," Jupiter said. "But when it was moved, naturally the street number would have been changed. I think I saw the marks where the old numbers were taken off."

"Oh? Then let's have another look. Make it as fast as you can."

Jupiter briefly pressed the button of the flashlight. A small circle of light focused on the numbers. And they all saw, just above the new numbers, marks in the paint where the old numbers had been. They were faint but clear.

"Number 532!" Pete exclaimed. "We've found it."

"Good work, Jupiter," Mr. Grant said. "Now let's get inside and find that money."

The door opened with a splintering noise, and they rushed into the living room. Bob found himself breathing fast with excitement. Now, for sure, they were right. Somewhere in this house fifty thousand dollars was pasted beneath the wallpaper.

"Give us some light, Jupiter," Mr. Grant said. Jupiter flashed the light on each wall in turn. The room was papered in a heavy raised design.

"It could easily be in here," the man said. "Rough wallpaper — easy to hide bills underneath it. Let's get to work."

Jupiter quickly made a cut and Mr. Grant turned the paper back. Underneath was only plaster wall.

"We'll start near the corner and work our way right around the room," Mr. Grant said. "Fifty thousand dollars in large bills wouldn't take up a whole wall. Let's make it snappy."

He and Jupiter had finished the first wall and started on the second, with Pete and Bob pressing close to watch, when a sudden noise made them freeze.

"What — " Mr. Grant began. He never finished the sentence. The front door was flung open and heavy feet came into the room with a rush. The beam of a large flashlight centered on the little group. And from behind the flashlight an ugly voice growled:

"All right, all of you! Put up your hands!"

WHERE IS THE MONEY?

They all turned, putting up their hands. The strong beam of light made them blink and squint and prevented them from seeing who was behind it.

"If you're the police," Mr. Grant started to say, "I'm George Grant, special investigator for —"

A brash laugh cut him short.

"George Grant! That's a good one. Is that what you told the kids?"

Jupiter blinked. A sudden sick realization came to him.

"Isn't he Mr. Grant, from the Bankers' Protective Association?" he asked.

"Him?" The deep, grating voice laughed again. "That's Smooth Simpson, one of the slickest cons in the business."

"But he has an official card," Pete protested.

"Sure he has. Printed special for him. He has a million of 'em. Don't feel bad if he fooled you. He's fooled the cops themselves plenty of times.

"Thought you could grab the cash right under our noses, didn't you, Smooth? But when the fat kid went into that junkyard and didn't come out again even when they closed, we knew something was up. We knew the house had to be over here someplace — got the info from the super of that apartment house after Fatty did yesterday — so we came here in a hurry. Spotted your light when you came into this house. Now we're here and we'll just take charge."

"You're Three-Finger Munger, aren't you?" Mr. Grant — or Smooth Simpson — said. "Listen, Three-Finger, why don't we all join forces? We haven't actually found the money yet, and I can help — "

"Shut up!" the man with the flashlight growled. "We'll find the money ourselves and leave you for the cops. Teach you not to try to pull a fast one on us. Now all of you turn around, face the wall. Put your hands behind your backs. No false moves or you'll regret it!

"Leo and Baby-Face, you got the ropes. Tie 'em up good."

With sinking hearts, The Three Investigators obeyed the orders. They realized now that they had been completely fooled by the slick criminal nicknamed Smooth. All his talk about Chief Reynolds had lulled any suspicions they might otherwise have had. He must have learned that the Chief was out of town for the day, and had then called The Three Investigators in a bold effort to trick them into telling anything they might know. And no wonder he had found excuses all along for not going to the police!

Mentally, Jupiter kicked himself for not suspecting something. But it had all been so plausible! Smooth was just that — smooth. No doubt he had read about the trunk in the newspaper, and knowing the story of the missing bank-robbery loot and Spike Neely's letter through underworld gossip, had started checking on Jupiter and the others. He could easily have gotten Jupiter's telephone number from Information or the phone book.

Three-Finger and his men had been following The Three Investigators, and Smooth Simpson had been following all of them!

But it was too late for any regrets. Deft hands were tying the boys' wrists behind their backs.

Moments later they were ordered to sit on the floor, and then their ankles were lashed together. When they were helpless, Three-Finger Munger chuckled.

"Now you look real pretty," he taunted them. "We won't gag you because there's nobody around to hear you if you yell. Anyway, if you act up, we'll clip you one on the head. Don't worry, someone will find you on Monday when work starts again. That is, I hope they'll find you before the bulldozers start knocking this house down."

He chuckled again. Now Jupiter and his companions could see that Three-Finger Munger was a burly man; his two associates were smaller. They could not see the faces of any of them clearly.

"Now let's see where we stand," Three-Finger said. He shone his light on the wall where Jupiter and Smooth had been working. "Looking for the money under the wallpaper, were you? That's a smart hiding place — never would have thought of it. Did the kid figure it out for you, Smooth?"

"Yes, he did," Smooth Simpson admitted. "The clue was on that letter Spike sent to Gulliver. It was in the trunk all along."

"I figured it had to be," Three-Finger said.

"That's why we wanted to get our hands on the trunk. My boys got it too, from that tall thin guy. Only somebody followed 'em and jumped 'em at the hideout and got it away before we could open it. Was that you, Smooth?"

"Not me," the man on the floor said. "I didn't know anything about that."

"Funny," Three-Finger muttered. "I wonder who it could have been. It certainly wasn't these kids."

"It was four or five guys with handkerchiefs over their faces," one of the other two said, speaking for the first time. "They were fast and tough. Laid us out before we knew what hit us."

"Wonder who it was?" Three-Finger grunted. "Maybe some other mob after the money. Well, the trunk didn't do them any good or they'd have been here before this. But we can't stand here talking. Leo, you and Baby-Face see what's under the wallpaper in the rest of the room."

The four captives on the floor watched silently as the two men swiftly slashed open the wallpaper on the remaining walls. Concerned as he was at their predicament, Jupiter could not help wondering who had seized Gulliver's trunk from these men and sent it back to him. But no answer to the riddle came to him. Meanwhile, Three-Finger's henchmen failed to find anything underneath the living-room wallpaper.

"Not in this room then," Three-Finger said. "Smooth, if you know which room it's in, better tell us. If you do, maybe we'll untie you when we're finished."

"If I knew I'd have gone straight for it," Smooth Simpson said. "But untie me and I'll help you find it."

"Not a chance," Three-Finger snapped. "You tried to grab the money from us and now you can pay for it. Come, fellows, we'll try the bedrooms."

The three thugs moved back to the first bedroom and left the four captives in darkness. The Three Investigators could hear them ripping at the wallpaper and cursing at their lack of success.

"Boys, I'm sorry this had to happen," Smooth Simpson said in a low tone. "I admit I tried to put a fast one over on you, but I didn't plan any violence. That's not how I work. I use brains, not force."

"It's my fault," Jupiter said, sounding unhappy. "I should have suspected you."

"Don't take it so hard," the man advised him. "I've fooled the best there are."

After that there was silence, except for the sounds from the rear of the house where Three-

Finger and his companions were at work. Then all four captives stiffened.

The front door had opened, creaking slightly!

Alertly, they all listened. Very faintly they could see the dark form of a rather small man ease into the room.

"Who's there?" Smooth demanded, keeping his voice to a whisper.

"Quiet!" came back an answering whisper. "We come to help. Don't let the others suspect anything."

Another man slipped in through the door, and a third. Still others followed. They could not be sure how many because of the darkness. The intruders were very skillful and made almost no noise.

"Men!" said the voice of the first. "Stay close to the walls, near the door. When they come out, get the bags over their heads and tie them up. No knives! Don't hurt them if you can help it."

A muffled grunt of understanding answered him.

Jupiter, Bob, and Pete waited with rising hope as well as bewilderment. Who could the men in the room be? They weren't the police, or they would have stormed in with lights and guns. Were they really friends? Or were they some other gang also after the hidden money?

Now the sound of angry voices from the rear indicated that Three-Finger and the others had failed to find the money. Their footsteps came down the hall to the dark living room. Three-Finger entered first, shining a light on the floor.

"All right, you fat kid!" he snarled at Jupiter. "We're through fooling. You tell us where that money is or else!"

STRUGGLE IN
THE DARKNESS

Suddenly Three-Finger was overwhelmed by several dark forms. Others grabbed the man behind and pulled him into the room. The third man tried to flee, but footsteps pounded after him and his muffled shouts indicated that he had been caught.

Meanwhile in the living room a terrific struggle followed. Three-Finger dropped his flashlight to the floor, where it rolled around, kicked by many feet, giving brief glimpses of the combat.

The Three Investigators could see that there was a bag over Three-Finger's head. Exerting his strength to the utmost, he threw off a couple

of his attackers, but others leaped on him. He
fell to the floor with a crash, and his companion
fell on top of him. They kicked and thrashed
about wildly.

"Quickly! Tie their hands and feet. Then gag
them!" ordered a voice.

For a moment longer the fight continued
furiously. Then Three-Finger and the others
were overpowered and bound. Three-Finger
began uttering violent threats, but these were
stilled as a gag was forced into his mouth. In a
moment he and the others were stretched out on
the floor, helpless. The only sound was the
heavy breathing of the men who had overpowered the criminals.

"Very good," said a friendly voice. "Wait outside. I will untie the boys."

The other men slipped quietly out the door,
leaving only one inside. This one turned on his
flashlight and shone it on the boys for a moment.

"Good." He chuckled. "No one fell on you and
smashed you flat. Now I set you free."

He placed the light on the floor so it would il-
luminate the boys without shining in their eyes.
Then he approached with a long knife. As he got
closer, Bob and Pete saw a swarthy man with a
fierce mustache, whom they had never seen be-

fore. But Jupiter recognized him.

"Lonzo!" he exclaimed. "The Gypsy from Zelda's house!"

Lonzo chuckled again as he cut the ropes that bound them.

"Yes," he said. "We meet once more."

"But — but how did you get here?" Jupiter asked in bewilderment as he stood up, rubbing his wrists.

"No time for talk now," the Gypsy said. "Where is the other one?"

He shone the light where Smooth Simpson had been. Smooth was missing. Two ropes lay on the floor.

"He got away!" Bob exclaimed. "He must have been quietly getting his hands free all along, and in the fight he slipped out!"

"He'll be far away by now," Lonzo said briefly. "No matter. We have three for the police. Now come outside. Zelda wishes to speak to you."

Zelda! The Gypsy fortune-teller! Jupiter followed Lonzo out the door, with Bob and Pete at his heels. Three old cars were parked at the curb. The two in the rear seemed to be crowded with men — Gypsies. In the front car a woman waited.

It was Zelda. She was not wearing Gypsy

clothes, perhaps to avoid attracting attention.

"They are all right, Zelda," Lonzo reported. "Three are tied up inside. One got away."

"No matter," Zelda said quietly. "Get in the car, boys, we must talk."

The three squeezed in with her. Lonzo remained on watch.

"So our paths cross again, Jupiter Jones," Zelda said. "It was written in the stars and in the crystal. I am glad we got here in time."

"Were you following us?" Jupiter asked as his thoughts began to clear.

"Yes," Zelda said. "Lonzo and some of the others were. Since first you visited me. The crystal said danger, and we wanted to prevent harm from coming to you. Lonzo followed those who followed you, and when they came here tonight, he sent for the rest of us to come to your aid. But we must be brief. You have found the money?"

"No," Jupiter sighed. "Apparently it isn't here. Yet I was positive the money was hidden in Spike's sister's house. The letter practically said so. That's the place it would logically be."

"Gulliver was sure the letter from Spike gave a clue to the hiding place, but he could not solve it," Zelda said.

"Then you knew Gulliver?" Jupiter asked.

"We are related," Zelda told him. "In an unusual way. I am anxious to clear his name and hoped that you, being very clever, could solve the mystery. Where did you look?"

"Under the wallpaper," Jupiter told her. "It's a place no one would think of. But it wasn't there."

"Why did you think it was?" Zelda asked.

"Well, Spike knew he couldn't actually *say* much in a letter," Jupiter explained. "He knew it would be censored. So he did something quite tricky, yet the only thing he could do."

"Well, boy, what was it?" Zelda sounded impatient. "Come, speak up."

It was Bob who answered.

"He did something peculiar with the stamps on the envelope. He put on two stamps, a two and a four. And he put a one-cent stamp, green, the color of money, under the four. We were positive he meant — "

"Bob, wait!" Jupiter called out.

Bob blinked. "What's the matter, First?" he asked.

"Say that again. The final words you just said."

"Why, all I said was that he put a one-cent stamp under the four and —"

"That's it!" Jupiter cried. "That's the clue!"

153

"What's the clue?" Pete put in. He and Bob and Zelda stared in puzzlement at Jupiter, whose face had suddenly become pink with excitement.

"Miss Zelda," Jupiter said, turning to the Gypsy woman, "Spike Neely had a slight speech defect. Chief Reynolds told us so. He had trouble pronouncing the letter L in some words."

"I believe that is true, boy," Zelda answered. "But what —"

"And his sister said Spike pronounced 'flower' as 'f'ower.' How would he pronounce 'floor'?"

"He'd pronounce it 'four,' " Zelda said after a moment. "Are you trying to tell me —"

"He put the money under the *floor*," Bob yelped. "He was sure Gulliver would remember his speech trouble and understand. Even if he didn't, 'four' and 'floor' sound enough alike to give the idea if you're looking for something tricky."

"Only we got carried away with the idea that he meant under the wallpaper, because Mrs. Miller told us Spike had papered the downstairs during his stay," Jupiter added excitedly. "Actually, I should have realized that pasting paper money under wallpaper is a bad idea — you'd never get it off again without ruining it. You'd have to scrape it off and that would be the end of

it. But safe and sound under the floor somewhere —"

"Lonzo!" Zelda ordered. "Get the tools from
the other car. We are going inside — you and I
and the boys."

A moment later they were crowding into the
house, ignoring the three bound prisoners on the
living-room floor. Consulting hastily, they
agreed that the living-room floor was unlikely.
Jupiter suggested that the right spot would either be under the floor in the guest room, where
Spike had stayed, or under the floor in the little
attic storage space.

They tried the attic first.

Ten minutes later Lonzo ripped up a board in
one corner — and Pete gave a shout.

There, in the beam of the flashlight, lay bundle after bundle of greenbacks, neatly stacked
between the joists of the first-floor ceiling!

"Under the four," Pete said, blinking. "Under
the *four*. What a smooth way to send a clue
when you knew a lot of people were going to
inspect your letter like hawks, looking for something. Jupe, you're the most!"

"I should have thought of it sooner," Jupiter
said. "Even if I didn't remember Spike Neely's
speech defect, I should have realized that 'four'
and 'floor' sound alike. And considering that

pasting money under wallpaper would ruin it, I —"

"Never mind, boy!" Zelda said. "You did a fine job. Gulliver himself did not suspect the truth. Now the money is found. The criminals are captured. The frog has jumped high and saved himself from the hungry fish in the pond."

She chuckled slightly. Jupiter looked as if he were suspecting a great deal that previously had been a mystery.

"You sent us that warning, Miss Zelda?" he asked.

The old Gypsy woman nodded.

"Indeed I did, boy. My Gypsies were keeping watch over you, but I wanted you to do your utmost to find the money — which you have. Now we must go. We will call the police, and the affair will be ended. You wait here for the police. They will take charge of the money and those crooks downstairs. The police will want to question us also, but they will not be able to find us. Not yet, at least."

"Wait, Zelda!" Jupiter said as the Gypsy woman and Lonzo turned to go. "Before you leave, I wish you would tell me something. About the trunk — how did it get back to us? And about the talking skull, Socrates — did he really talk or —"

"Later, later," the woman said. "In two weeks visit me at the old address. We will then have returned. Your questions will be answered."

"But at least tell us about Gulliver," Jupiter urged. "Where is he?"

"I thought he was dead," Pete put in.

"I did not say so," Zelda replied. "I said he had vanished from the world of men. Now, perhaps he may return from the world where he has been. For two weeks — farewell."

With that, she and Lonzo hurried down the stairs and The Three Investigators heard the Gypsies' cars roar away into the night. The three looked at each other, and Bob gave a sigh of relief.

"Wow!" he said. "We did it, Jupe! We found the missing money!"

"With some help from Zelda," Jupiter said. "I'm certainly looking forward to seeing her again. I have a hunch she can give me some very interesting answers!"

ALFRED HITCHCOCK ASKS SOME QUESTIONS

Alfred Hitchcock, the noted motion-picture producer, sat behind the desk in his office and leafed through the many pages of notes regarding the mystery of the talking skull, which had been prepared by Bob Andrews. Then he glanced across to where The Three Investigators, in their best clothes, sat in a row and waited for him to speak.

"Excellently done, lads," Alfred Hitchcock rumbled. "Jupiter, my boy, you did well to locate the missing money, after the authorities failed for so long."

But Jupiter's round features looked glum.

"No, sir," he sighed. "I should have solved the secret sooner. First, I thought that one stamp being under the other meant the money was pasted under some wallpaper. I should have known better and looked for the other meaning. Then, if it hadn't been for some luck —"

"Luck helps those who are alert," Mr. Hitchcock said. "As I have reminded you before. You can't expect to get the right answer the very first thing every time — no investigator manages that. In my opinion you did very well."

"Thank you, sir." Jupiter brightened. "Anyway, we did find the missing money."

"And none too soon, either," the director remarked. "Two days later the house would have been bulldozed to the ground and the money might easily have been lost forever in the wreckage. Tell me, did you collect the reward?"

Jupiter sighed. Pete sighed. Bob sighed.

"No, sir," Bob said. "There wasn't really any reward — that was just a story Smooth Simpson made up, along with all the rest he told us. But we did get a very nice letter from the bank president, and Chief Reynolds said he wished we were old enough to be on his force as detectives."

"Ah, well, money is not the only reward for a job well done," commented Mr. Hitchcock. "Now, I have a question or two. I believe these notes make clear how Spike Neely hid the money in the first place, and how he managed to get a very secret message out of the prison hospital to his friend, Gulliver — so secret, of course, that no one could solve it until it fell into your hands.

"But my first question, and one your notes do not answer, is what became of Gulliver. What was his fate?"

The boys grinned. They had been expecting Mr. Hitchcock to ask, and Jupiter was prepared with the answer.

"When he got the letter from Spike Neely," Jupiter said, "Gulliver suspected Spike was trying to send him a message, because in prison Spike had said he would tell the secret to Gulliver if anything ever happened to him. However, Gulliver couldn't solve the message. So he hid the letter in his trunk.

"Then one day as he was coming back to his hotel, the clerk told him some men had been asking for him. He recognized the description of Three-Finger Munger and he became very frightened. He knew that Three-Finger might easily kidnap him and torture him to find out where the money was, and of course Gulliver didn't know. If he had known, he'd have directed the authorities to it. In any case, he wasn't sure whether the police would believe his story.

"So without even going up to his room, Gulliver just vanished. He left everything. His trunk was put into storage when he didn't return, and eventually sold at public auction. To me."

"Then Gulliver didn't die?" Mr. Hitchcock asked sharply. "But the Gypsy, Zelda, told you that he had vanished from the world of men."

"Which is what he did," Jupiter said, his grin becoming broader. "He wanted to be sure Three-Finger Munger and his pals couldn't possibly find him. So he dressed up as a woman and put on a wig. He became a woman in appearance and that way vanished from the world of men."

"Of course!" Mr. Hitchcock exclaimed. "I should have guessed that's what the words meant. Now — a thought is coming to me. Let me see if I too can deduce correctly. I deduce that the Gypsy woman, Zelda, was really The Great Gulliver!"

Pete chuckled. So did Bob. Jupiter nodded his head.

"That's right, sir," he said. "The Gypsies were old friends of Gulliver's. In fact, his mother had been a Gypsy. They let him come and live with them. And of course Gypsies are very clannish, so they never betrayed his secret."

Now Alfred Hitchcock too chuckled.

"Well," he said. "One mystery solved. Obviously Gulliver, who used to be plump, dieted himself thin and knew that no one would ever dream that a thin Gypsy woman was really a missing fat magician. What are his plans now?"

"He'll stop being Zelda soon and become himself again," Jupiter said. "As soon as Three-Finger Munger and his friends are safely in prison. But he's not going to become a magician again. The Gypsies have come to depend on him to handle their business affairs and he's going to stay with them."

"I see." Alfred Hitchcock went back through Bob's notes to the beginning. "Ah hah!" he said. "I see that when you bought the trunk at auction, Jupiter, a little old lady came rushing in, very excited, and wanted to buy it, but was too late. By any chance, was that — ?"

"Yes, sir. That was Gulliver, wearing a different wig and dressed as an elderly lady. He kept track of such sales and managed to learn that his trunk was going up for sale. But he had the time wrong and was too late.

"He would have tried harder to buy it from us, but that reporter appeared with a camera, and Gulliver was afraid of attracting attention. The story in the newspaper, though, told him who we were and how to find us."

"It also told Three-Finger Munger and his pals," Pete put in darkly.

"Yes," Jupiter agreed. "First Three-Finger Munger's men tried to steal the trunk. Later on they did steal it, by following Maximilian the Mystic and running his car off the road. But they didn't keep it long.

"You see, Mr. Hitchcock, as Zelda said, the Gypsies were keeping an eye on us. When she — I mean Gulliver — learned we had actually solved some difficult mysteries, he got the idea that we might solve the secret of where the money was hidden. We would lead the police to it, and then he could reappear.

"That's why he had me come down to meet him, as Zelda, and talked in a mysterious way to get me interested. Then the Gypsies spotted Three-Finger and his pals, and when they stole the trunk from Maximilian, a carful of Gypsies was right behind them. The Gypsies followed the thieves to their hideout, jumped on them, and got the trunk away before the crooks knew what hit them.

"Then Zelda — that is, Gulliver — sent the

trunk back to me, still hoping I'd manage to solve the mystery. In fact, he knew I almost had to in order to get rid of Three-Finger and the others. So he had the Gypsies keep a close eye on us, so they could help us if we needed them.

"That Saturday night when Smooth Simpson tricked us into helping him find Mrs. Miller's lost house, the Gypsies were watching Three-Finger. They didn't know about Smooth Simpson. When Three-Finger and his gang started out, they followed. When Three-Finger made us prisoners, they sent for reinforcements and were in time to rescue us and grab the Three-Finger mob.

"Then — well, you know how we finally found the money."

Mr. Hitchcock nodded. He made a steeple of his fingers and looked across it at the boys.

"Now then," he said. "For the final question. Did Socrates, the talking skull, really talk? And if he did, how? What was the secret? And I will not accept any supernatural explanations."

"No, sir," Jupiter said. "I mean the explanation isn't supernatural. Everything a magician does is really a trick, of course, and Socrates was a trick too. Gulliver is a good ventriloquist. In the beginning he used ventriloquism to make Socrates talk.

"Then, when people began to suspect him, he figured out a way to make Socrates talk from a distance. He bought a tiny sending and receiving radio device — you know they can make them very small now —"

"And installed it inside the skull?" Mr. Hitchcock frowned. I would certainly have expected you to detect that, Jupiter. I believe you examined the skull thoroughly and could hardly have missed it."

"That's just it, sir," Jupiter explained. "I did examine Socrates carefully. That's where Gulliver was clever. He put the device inside the ivory *base*, where it couldn't be seen."

"Ah!" the director said. "Inside the base where it wouldn't be seen or suspected. A clever touch. But please continue."

"The transmitter inside the base was voice-operated," Jupiter went on. "That means that after we had taken Socrates out of the trunk and put him on the base, anything we said would be broadcast. The range was about five hundred feet.

"Gulliver, disguised as a woman — not a Gypsy woman — was hanging around the salvage yard after he learned where the trunk had gone. He had a little speaker in his ear, hidden by his wig, and a microphone in an ornamental pin on his dress. He could hear us talking. He didn't intend to speak to us then, but he unexpectedly sneezed. That's how we heard Socrates seem to sneeze.

"Then that night when I kept Socrates in my room, Gulliver was hiding nearby. He saw my lights go out and took a chance on speaking to me through Socrates. That was when he gave me the mysterious message to go down and see Zelda.

"The next day, when Aunt Mathilda was cleaning in my room and telling Socrates what she thought of him, Gulliver was listening and couldn't resist saying 'Boo!' to her."

"So the mystery is explained," commented Mr. Hitchcock. "It was really The Great Gulliver at all times. Indeed, a case of science rather than superstition."

"Yes, sir," Jupiter nodded. "And as we usually had Socrates nearby when we were talking about the case, Gulliver could listen in on our progress and plans. That way he knew pretty much everything we were doing. That made it a lot easier for him to keep an eye on us and come to our rescue in the end."

"All in all, a most interesting case," the director said. "Well, I will be glad to introduce it for you, as I have your others. Have you any idea what you'll work on next?"

"Not yet," Jupiter said as they all rose. "But we're keeping our eyes open. We'll be in touch with you, Mr. Hitchcock."

They filed out of the office, and the director smiled to himself. A talking skull! What would they come up with next time!